MR FITTON AND THE BLACK LEGION

By the same author

HMS *Cracker*
Gun-Brig Captain
The Lee Shore
Stella and the Fireships
Mutiny in the Caribbean
Seven-Gun Broadside
The Quarterdeck Ladder
A Sword for Mr Fitton
Mr Fitton's Commission
The Baltic Convoy
Nelson's Midshipman
A Ship for Mr Fitton
The Independent Cruise
Mr Fitton's Prize

SHOWELL STYLES

Mr Fitton and the Black Legion

ROBERT HALE · LONDON

© Showell Styles 1994
First published in Great Britain 1994

ISBN 0 7090 5301 0

Robert Hale Limited
Clerkenwell House
Clerkenwell Green
London EC1R 0HT

The right of Showell Styles to be identified as
author of this work has been asserted by him
in accordance with the Copyright, Designs and
Patents Act 1988.

C 120422293

Photoset in North Wales by
Derek Doyle & Associates, Mold, Clwyd.
Printed in Great Britain by
St Edmundsbury Press Ltd, Bury St Edmunds, Suffolk.
Bound by WBC Ltd, Bridgend, Mid-Glamorgan.

Contents

1	Colonel Tate	7
2	Winter Journey	31
3	Secret Emissary	57
4	The Sporting Shot	81
5	Invasion	103
6	Pencaer by Moonlight	131
7	The Hostage	153
8	Quixote at Fishguard	175
	Author's Note	189

1   Colonel Tate

1

Michael Fitton knew that he was about to die. In boarding the French corvette, cutlass in hand, he had stumbled and fallen on hands and knees. The steel point of a boarding-pike was a foot from his throat and the unshaven face of the Frenchman behind it wore a savage grin of triumph.

After that flash of realization it seemed to Mr Fitton that time stood still and the uproar of shots and yells around him ceased. He felt a surge of emotion; not fear but an angry disgust that he should have to die in the moment of victory. The corvette, outgunned and outnumbered, was bound to strike.

There was a shout and a clatter and the din of the fight was in his ears again. The boarding-pike had fallen to the deck and so had the Frenchman behind it, his head split open by a cutlass slash. Mr Fitton felt himself seized by the collar of his coat and jerked to his feet. He saw the man who had saved him rush on with his reddened cutlass raised and plunge into the mob of struggling men at the foot of the corvette's mainmast, a big man with a mop of tow-coloured hair. So it was to Tom Evans, one of *Iris*'s four leading seamen, that he owed his life. He tightened his grip of the cutlass-hilt and sprang forward to take his place with the frigate's fighting-men, stepping over two blood-draggled bodies as he went.

But he was too late. Overborne by the impetus and numbers of the frigate's boarding-party, the French seamen were penned against the corvette's lee rail, and their leader, a small man with an epaulette on his left shoulder, was shrieking that they surrendered. The voice of Collins, *Iris*'s first lieutenant, thundered above the tumult.

'Lay off! Lay off, there! Get back, damn you!'

Frenchmen and Englishmen drew apart, the distortions wrought by hand-to-hand conflict fading from their faces. Three men lay in their blood on the open space of deck between them, and a broad-shouldered seaman with a thatch of greying hair was kneeling beside one of the bodies.

' 'Nother 'arf-minute and 'e'd bin standin' 'ere with us, pore sod,' said a man beside Mr Fitton.

'Ran straight on some bugger's sword,' said another. 'I seed him.'

The grey-haired man stood up and came to join his messmates, his weather-beaten face grimly set. It was Sam Evans, Tom's elder brother and also a leading seaman.

'Dead,' he said briefly.

To Mr Fitton the grey January afternoon seemed to darken, and the thin drizzle that blew across the slow Atlantic waves chilled his cheek. He was punctilious in paying his debts, and here was a debt he could never repay.

'Mr Fraser!' Collins was shouting. 'See to it that every Frog's disarmed. Weapons aft here. Reeves, take six hands and get our dead and wounded aboard *Iris*. Larboard watch, secure all guns –'

Mr Fitton, who was a master's mate and not one of the larboard watch, stuck his unused cutlass in his belt and looked around him in the fading light. The frigate lay alongside her beaten opponent, her side considerably higher than the corvette's rail and her reefed topsails flapping wetly in the light wind. A ragged hole in the foretopsail was the only visible sign of the running fight that had preceded the corvette's capture, but he knew that *Iris*'s hull had been hit more than once, on her waterline or near it. As that thought crossed his mind a rhythmic *clank-clank-clank* began to sound from the frigate; already Captain Newnham had started her pumps.

'Hoist away!'

The Union flag soared up to the corvette's masthead, taking the place of the French colours which had just been hauled down. Collins, red-faced and bull-necked, doffed his cocked hat as it rose and then swung round to survey the busy deck. A rank of marines, their red jackets blotched with wet and their muskets at the ready, held the packed mass of French seamen up for'ard, and their lieutenant was running aft.

'Get 'em under hatches, Mr Collins?'

'No. Send your sergeant and four men below to search the messdecks for skulkers first.' The first lieutenant's glance swept round. 'Here, you – Mr Fitton! Dreaming of your bloody earldom? Take two hands and search the after cabins, and look lively!'

'Aye, aye, sir.'

'Craigie, Evans, you'll go with him.'

Mr Fitton walked briskly to the companion-hatch with the two seamen at his heels. He felt no resentment at the gibe. Collins had somehow discovered that he was the last – and penniless – scion of the Fittons of Gawsworth, a family older than Magna Carta, and he lost no opportunity of derisive reminder.

It was dark on the steep ladder of steps. Halfway down Mr Fitton paused to speak over his shoulder.

'I'm sorry about your brother, Evans.'

'Aye, sir.' Sam Evans's deep voice was steady. 'Died

doin' his duty, though. Tis a good way out.'

The darkening afternoon could not light the alleyway at the foot of the steps but a lantern glimmered on the bulkhead by the open door of the arms store, left there no doubt when weapons had been served out to repel boarders. Mr Fitton lifted it from its hook and they proceeded with their search, while the corvette's wooden hull echoed with the shouts and banging of the marines going through the messdecks for'ard. Since she had no raised quarterdeck the corvette's after cabins were all below deck level, officers' quarters on either side of the alleyway and captain's right aft amidships. They had searched the alleyway cabins and found all of them empty when Craigie spoke suddenly.

'There's noises, sir – larboard side aft.'

Mr Fitton, who had been casting his lantern light into the empty midships cabin, stood still and listened. A voice, throaty and slow-spoken, came to his ear from the small cabin to larboard of the captain's.

'That's an English voice or I'm a nigger. In here, friends!'

He pushed open the cabin door and went in, his lantern held high. A man was sitting with his legs up on the bunk under the low deckhead, a lean elderly man in brown coat and breeches and white stockings. His ankles were lashed together with cord and his long thin fingers were writhing in an attempt to throw off the loosened coils of line that had bound his wrists. He succeeded, with a 'Hah!' of triumph, as they came in.

'If I'd gotten my hands free ten minutes ago,' he remarked coolly, 'I'd not have to ask what's eventuated, sir.' He pronounced the last word *suh*. 'I reckon this vessel's been chased and captured by a British ship. Is that so?'

The lantern light accentuated the furrows of a bony face whose skin had a yellowish tinge. A big beaky nose jutted above an inordinately long chin, and the pale eyes, that flickered restlessly from one to another of the three who stood regarding him, were very bright for a man whose lank hair was almost white.

'First, if you please, your name and how you come to be here,' Mr Fitton said evenly.

'My name, sir, is Tate, Colonel William Tate, lately of the fourth Regiment, South Carolina Line.' The drawling voice held a hint of bombast. 'And I have the pleasure of addressing –'

'Fitton, master's mate in His Majesty's frigate *Iris*, sir. Evans, cast off those lashings from his feet. How comes it, colonel, that a citizen of the United States is held prisoner aboard a French corvette?'

'Thankee, friend.' Colonel Tate swung his freed legs off the bunk and bent to massage his ankles. 'Prisoner is correct, sir. I have been hog-tied here for better than an hour, and I declare I am considerable used up. As to how I come –' He straightened himself with a jerk, 'What the Eternal is that?'

A sudden reverberant thunder, punctuated by shouted orders, was shaking the cabin bulkheads.

'That's our prisoners being sent down to the forehold,' Mr Fitton said. 'Nigh on two hundred of them. Legitimate prisoners of war,' he added without alteration of tone.

Colonel Tate darted an amused glance at him. 'Aiming to say I was tied up here illegally? Not so, sir, not so. My nation may be neutral in this conflict but there are such things as soldiers of fortune, sir, and I take leave to call myself one of them. I was on my way to offer my services to your Government when my purpose was discovered and I was taken.'

'But that doesn't explain –'

Mr Fitton was checked by a solemnly uplifted hand. With his deeply lined face and long white hair the colonel looked like a Hebrew prophet pronouncing a blessing.

'Excuse me, Mr – Fitton, was it? – excuse me if I draw your attention to my rank and to yours. A colonel, I opinionate, may be required to explain himself to no one below the naval rank of captain.' He cocked his head on one side. 'Am I correct, sir?'

'You are correct, sir,' Mr Fitton echoed gravely. 'I offer my apologies. You shall be presented to Captain Newnham at the first opportunity. You have some baggage?'

Colonel Tate stood up, stooping under the low deckhead. Despite the stoop it was evident that he was at least as tall as Sam Evans, who topped six feet, though Evans had nearly twice his breadth.

'I travel light, Mr Fitton,' he said. 'My valise is in the corner yonder, and hat and cloak is all I have else.'

He took a heavy black cloak and a black three-cornered hat from a hook on the bulkhead as he spoke, and draped the cloak on his narrow shoulders.

'Bring that valise, Craigie,' said Mr Fitton. 'Please to follow me, sir.'

He could hear Collins bellowing his name as they climbed the companion-ladder. On deck parties of seamen were working furiously to get *Iris*'s prize ready for sailing, and there was not a Frenchman to be seen.

'By God you took your time, Mr Fitton!' Collins rasped as they approached. 'Let's have your report.' His eye fell on Colonel Tate. 'Who the devil's this?'

'Aye aye, sir,' said Mr Fitton briskly. 'All after cabins searched, one person found – this gentleman. He was tied up, a prisoner. He says he is Colonel William Tate, United States citizen, and requests to see the captain.'

'He does, does he?' The first lieutenant glared uncertainly at the colonel and apparently decided on politeness. 'You'll pardon me, sir, but I've my hands full at present. This vessel has to be got under way at once – captain's orders.' He turned and shouted. 'Mr Fitzroy!'

A diminutive midshipman detached himself from one

of the working-parties and came running aft. Collins pointed to the colonel.

'Take Colonel Tate on board *Iris*, Mr Fitzroy, and report to Captain Newnham. And look sharp!' he added explosively. 'What are you waiting for?'

'If you p-please, sir,' piped the midshipman nervously, 'number four gun's off its carriage and we can't get it back.'

Collins swung round on Mr Fitton. 'Take your men for'ard and lend a hand with that gun.'

By the time the colonel and his youthful escort had climbed aboard the frigate, Sam Evans's phenomenal strength had turned the scale and the 12-pounder was back on its carriage.

'By'r leave, sir,' Sam muttered as they turned away together. 'Seemed to me you was a mite doubtful consarnin' this Colonel Tate.'

'Well?'

'Well, sir – them lashin's on his ankles. No seaman, French or English, tied the knots. A pair o' grannies, an' loose at that.'

Mr Fitton said nothing. But he had noted that the door of Colonel Tate's cabin was unlocked, and that the key was in the lock on the inside of the door. There were, he reflected, one or two things that were a little odd about Colonel William Tate.

2

HMS *Iris* was a 32-gun frigate, one of the earliest of a class the Admiralty had ceased building long before the war with France had begun four years ago. Though a fast sailer she was nearly due for the ship-breaker's yard, which (Mr Fitton had concluded) was why she had been assigned to the winter blockade of Brest. Their Lordships were not going to subject their newest ships to the wear and tear of ceaseless patrol off the mouth of the Iroise in December and January. So for more than two months of stormy weather *Iris*, with two other elderly frigates, had been beating to and fro across the wind-tossed waters south of Ushant, keeping watch over the French fleet, 22 ships of the line, that lay in the Rade de Brest. Admiral Colpoys and his squadron of battleships lay eight leagues out in the Atlantic, awaiting the frigates' report if the French should sail.

In Mr Fitton's considered but unexpressed opinion, eight leagues was much too great a distance for a successful interception, and in the event he was proved right. Repeated easterly gales drove patrols and squadron far out beyond their stations, and four days before Christmas a French fleet sailed from Brest without opposition, 17 ships of the line with transports carrying 15,000 troops. This expedition was bound for Ireland and a subsequent invasion of England across St George's Channel, which could hardly have failed to succeed against the few hundred half-trained militia in Wales and the west of England. Only the weather defeated them. Fierce east winds laden with sleet and snow drove them out of Bantry Bay without disembarking their troops and they returned to France, losing three ships on the way.

The first news *Iris*'s crew heard of this near-disaster came from *Pomona*, the frigate sent out from Portsmouth to relieve them towards the end of January. Relief was certainly due. *Iris*'s canvas was threadbare, her much-spliced rigging was chafed in a score of places, and her ancient timbers were creaking like an old man's bones. As for her men, they were sick of the ceaseless pounding through stormy seas with nothing to show for it – no action with the enemy – no taking of prizes – and there was universal satisfaction on board when the frigate, having made 2 leagues of westing to clear Ushant, turned her bows north-north-east to begin the

250-mile voyage to Portsmouth. Mr Fitton, though his square brown face as usual showed no emotion, was happier than he had been for many weeks past.

He had joined *Iris*, obedient to orders, in February of 1796, and he had never liked her. For fifteen years, nearly half his life, ships had been home to Mr Fitton; he had no other. But he could not succeed in feeling at home in *Iris*. Her captain, Newnham, was a brash youngster of twenty-two who (it was rumoured) had gained his position by influence, and he was no seaman. Collins, first lieutenant, was a good seaman beyond doubt, but from the first he had vented an inexplicable dislike of the new master's mate in stinging sarcasms. The crew was the usual mixture of man-o'-war's men like Tom and Sam Evans and pressed landsmen from Portsmouth; and the warrant-officers with whom Mr Fitton messed had no special defects; yet the ease of familiar company and surroundings had never settled upon him in *Iris*. He had not allowed this unease to weigh heavily upon him, however. Mr Fitton was a disciple of the Stoic philosopher Epictetus, who had said 'Fortify yourself with contentment, for contentment is an impregnable fortress'. He had tried, not ineffectually, to be contented; but he was glad to be heading for Portsmouth. It was next to certain that *Iris* would be sent into dock for refit, in which case he would be transferred to another ship.

They had been three leagues north of Ushant, in milder weather with a moderate sea, when *Iris* had sighted the French corvette and Captain Newnham had ordered the chase that had ended in her capture. Mr Fitton had his own opinion about that brief action. *Iris*, the faster vessel, carried 18-pounder long guns with an effective range of nearly a mile; the corvette's broadside consisted of shorter-range 12-pounder carronades capable of inflicting heavy damage at close quarters. In Newnham's place, Mr Fitton would have kept beyond the Frenchman's range and used his 18-pounders until she was dismasted and forced to strike. Instead, Newnham had chosen to close and board, thereby exposing his ship for a few vital minutes to that smashing broadside. There had been few casualties; Tom Evans was the only British seaman to be killed, while the French had lost four men including their captain. But the frigate had been seriously damaged. As she resumed her northerly course with her prize, the corvette *Garonne*, following astern, her pumps were hard at work expelling the water that spurted in through her shattered side. Their metallic thudding sounded loudly in the wooden box of a cabin to which Mr Fitton descended at the end of his watch-on-deck.

Of the four men with whom he shared the warrant officers' mess, two – boatswain and carpenter – were absent on deck. The other two were sitting at the little table talking by the light of the oil-lamp in its gimbals on the bulkhead. Mr Judd the gunner sat frowning and rubbing his bristly chin, while Mr Lecky, captain's secretary, did most of the talking. Lecky glanced up briefly as Mr Fitton hung his wet oilskin on its hook and seated himself, but his voice flowed on uninterruptedly. He was a thin-faced little man, prematurely bald, and he loved the sound of that voice. It was being kept very low just now; in recounting what had passed in the captain's cabin half an hour ago he was contravening naval regulations.

'I'm telling you what he told the captain, Mr Judd,' he was saying. 'It's not for me to adjudicate whether it's true or false. Posing as an inquiring American wishful to see the new Republic, he was. His real aim was to get to England with the information he'd collected. Letters of introduction he's got, from nobs in the United States government – he showed 'em to the captain.'

'Intaduction to the Frogs?' Judd growled.

'No, no – to our nobs in London.'

'This Colonel Tate's a spy, then?'

'Your guess is as good as mine, Mr Judd. I'm just telling you what he said while I was sitting by taking notes for the captain. He said he reckons the French got wind of his real intentions while he was in Brest, because this smuggling brig he'd arranged to board at Roscoff hadn't made more than a few leagues when up comes this corvette –'

'What time o' day was this?' the gunner demanded.

'Why, this very morning, just before noon.'

'An' the brig was to take him to England?'

' 'Course she was. Why?'

Judd shook his head. 'She couldn't ha' been on course for England, Mr Lecky. By what you've just said, this Colonel Tate was a hundred mile east of us at noon an' we sighted the corvette – him in it, d'ye see – at six bells arternoon watch. No man could travel a hundred mile in three hours, brig or corvette.'

Mr Fitton, who had been listening with interest, joined the conversation. 'The brig could have been blown off course. The easterly was blowing hard until noon.'

'She was blown a bloody long way, then,' Judd said.

'Be that as it may,' Lecky said impatiently, 'an officer and two hands from the corvette came aboard the brig and took Colonel Tate off – they let the brig go. He was put in a cabin with a guard on the door. Later on a seaman came in and tied him up – he thinks that must have been when *Iris* was sighted.'

'What did Captain Newnham say to all this?' asked Mr Fitton curiously.

'Welcomed him with open arms,' said Lecky. 'He's to have Mr Fraser's cabin and dine with the captain. When we reach Portsmouth he's to be put in the way of getting to London quick as possible. That'll be post-chaise –'

He stopped as a mess-boy came in with a steaming covered dish. The gunner sniffed at it disgustedly.

'Same old dead horse,' he growled. 'Juicy steak runnin' with gravy – that's my mark when we get to Portsmouth.'

But Mr Judd was not to eat his juicy steak at Portsmouth. At two bells of the first watch *Iris* and her prize altered course to northward, and everyone on board knew they were heading for Plymouth.

This change of destination did not surprise Mr Fitton. With the coming of the milder rainy weather the wind had backed and was now blowing a fresh breeze from the south-east; on a course for Portsmouth *Iris* would be continuously heeled to larboard, the leaks on her waterline below the level of the waves. Not only the lesser heel on a northerly course but also the shorter distance would have influenced Captain Newnham's decision – no doubt he had been advised by his first lieutenant. They would hardly reach the home port in less than two days' sailing, whereas if the wind held they could be in Plymouth Sound before nightfall of next day. Mr Fitton was looking forward to seeing Plymouth, for none of the ships in which he had served had put in there. The dockyard, he had heard, had recently been enlarged, though it was far from being a great naval base like Portsmouth. Would he get the chance of a run ashore, he wondered? Or would he be drafted straight away to another ship? Two hundred and thirty men beside himself were wondering the same.

The wind held steady over the frigate's starboard quarter, and when Mr Fitton came up to take over the deck for the middle watch it had stopped raining. His rating of master's mate entitled him to act as officer of the watch if need arose, and since Mr Fraser the second lieutenant had been put in charge of the prize he had been ordered to take his place. Except for the duty midshipman, a huddled figure in the corner by the taffrail, he had the quarterdeck to himself. There was no moon behind the low clouds and the mizenmast with its four dark sails towered into obscurity overhead. Below him, at the foot of the quarterdeck ladder, a faint radiance from the windows of the captain's cabin, where a marine sentry stood guard, fell on the deck planking. Just for'ard of it was the only other light, the glow from the binnacle lamp under the eye of the helmsman. From for'ard, just audible above the sounds of wind and wave, came the buzz of low-voiced talk among the men of the duty watch. Mr Fitton was as nearly solitary as a man can be in a crowded warship. He began to pace up and down the weather side of the quarterdeck.

His thoughts reverted to that conversation in the warrant officers' mess two hours ago. The point Judd had made was a good one and it matched the other oddnesses he had noticed about Colonel Tate, small things that didn't quite fit in with the story he told. These small matters would fit neatly enough into another story. Suppose the *Garonne* to have sailed from Brest — a vessel of her size could easily slip out through the Raz de Sein — with the purpose of landing Colonel Tate secretly on the English coast, Tate being an agent in French pay. Suppose Tate, perceiving that the corvette was about to be taken by an English frigate, to have tied himself up in his cabin to give colour to the tale he had quickly concocted. All the inconsistencies — the unlikely place where he had been taken off the 'smuggling brig', the unlocked cabin door, the unseamanlike knots, the fact that his valise and his letters of introduction had not been taken from him — all these vanished in this different version of Tate's activities. As for the letters of introduction, such things could be forged, or so Mr Fitton had heard.

He turned at the rail in his pacing and as he did so the double clang of two bells, an hour after midnight, sounded from the deck below. That smuggling brig, now. *Garonne*'s captain would have known the truth about that, but he was dead; and the other officers of the corvette had refused to give any information beyond their names and ranks, according to the rules of naval warfare. Her crew would know, though. At Plymouth, perhaps he might make an opportunity of questioning –

Mr Fitton pulled himself up short. What was he about? Captain Newnham had accepted Tate, had seen his credentials, was responsible for the American's bona fides. The suspicions (for they were no more) of a master's mate were of no account in the matter, and in any case they could all be explained away: the brig blown off course, the knots tied hastily in the heat of a running fight, the door left unlocked when the sentry rushed on deck to repel the boarders. It was none of his business, and he might as well forget about it.

A burst of laughter came to his ears from for'ard, followed instantly by a stern command that silenced it. That was Sam Evans's voice; there was never any trouble with the duty watch when Leading Seaman Evans was in charge of it. It had been decided, he remembered, that Sam's brother Tom should be buried at sea, at the end of the forenoon watch. Mr Fitton halted in his pacing and stood staring into the blackness astern, where the spreading pallor of the frigate's wake vanished towards the invisible corvette. He was considering his debt.

In the long months of battling with the winter storms off the Iroise he had become aware that *Iris* had two outstanding seamen amongst her hard-worked crew. The brothers Evans, he had discovered, hailed from a small fishing port on the coast of Pembrokeshire, where they had learned the way of ships and the sea almost as soon as they could walk. Sometimes they spoke to each other in Welsh, but long service on the lower deck had robbed their English speech of its Welsh accent, though in moments of stress they would rip out what was presumably a Welsh oath. Tom, the younger brother, was a big man, but Sam was a bigger man still and cooler in emergencies. Unusually for a British seaman, he was a fine swimmer. Mr Fitton had seen him save the life of a hand who had gone overboard in a rough sea off the Pointe du Raz, plunging from the rail without a second's hesitation and supporting the man amid the tossing wave-caps while the frigate brought-to and lowered a boat. He had admired and liked both men. And now Tom was dead and he owed Tom his life.

He turned abruptly to go for'ard, stopping as he remembered that he should not leave the quarterdeck unnecessarily and there was a duty midshipman to carry messages.

'Mr Snape, go for'ard, if you please, and pass the order for Evans to come aft.'

'Aye aye,' responded the midshipman, detaching himself from his corner.

Mr Fitton noted the omission of the *sir*, to which he was entitled, without rancour. Despite the added step of his master's mate rating he was, he knew, really no more than a senior midshipman; and he knew also that the coveted lieutenant's commission, though denied to him by a series of ill chances, was also delayed by sundry independent actions of his own which had displeased his senior officers. His present duties made him in effect an acting lieutenant, but there was no likelihood of that rank being confirmed in *Iris*.

'Sir,' said the big man who had come up the ladder to stand before him.

'A word with you, Evans.' Mr Fitton drew him to the weather-rail, out of earshot of Snape who had retired to his corner. 'You may not know it, but your brother saved my life aboard the corvette. There was a pike at my breast when he cut the Frenchman down and got me on my feet.'

'I'm glad o' that, sir. Tom was ever quick with his blow.'

'I'd like to show my gratitude in some way. Is there

anything I can do? See your parents, for instance, if I get leave. Your home's at – what was the name of the place?'

'Fishguard, sir. But I've no home there now, and Mam and Dad have been dead these six years. Thankee, all the same.'

'No relations?' Mr Fitton persisted.

Sam hesitated. 'There's Uncle Evan at Letterston, which is four mile south out o' Fishguard, but me an' Tom's not seen him since we was lads.'

'Well, bear in mind what I've said. You'll understand, Evans – I can't repay a debt like that but I'd feel more comfortable if there was something – anything – I could do.'

'I understand, sir. And I'll bear it in mind.'

From the darkness for'ard came a flap and a clatter.

'Lee mainsheet's slack,' said Mr Fitton. 'Take a turn on it.'

'Aye aye, sir,' said Evans, and disappeared down the quarterdeck ladder.

Mr Fitton resumed his pacing. The tilted deck under his feet suddenly began to vibrate with the monotonous clanking of the pumps. They hadn't been worked for more than an hour so *Iris* was not taking in a hazardous amount of water. Under plain sail she was making six or seven knots, so she was likely to reach Plymouth well before sunset – Plymouth, where he might find himself transferred to another ship or put ashore to await draft in a naval barracks. He was able to view either prospect with equability. 'Require not things to happen as you wish, but wish them to happen as they do happen, and you will go on well.' Epictetus was a sound guide for any sea officer.

3

'We therefore commit his body to the deep,' Captain Newnham mumbled, and closed his book.

The men holding the grating on the lee rail tilted it sharply, and the shot-weighted hammock slid overboard into the waves racing alongside. The captain turned away, recollected himself, and paused to raise his cocked hat briefly, and then made for his cabin. The first lieutenant's bellow dismissed the assembled hands. Tom Evans's body had returned to the element that had nursed him and found him work since he was a boy.

Mr Fitton dodged through the dispersing seamen and found a comparatively retired spot at the rail by the break of the poop. It was his watch below but he could stay on deck if he wanted to, and in the astonishingly mild weather of this winter day, with a pale sun appearing now and then behind the racing clouds, the deck was no longer the icy purgatory it had been a week ago. The wind had backed still farther and freshened, raising a choppy sea and driving *Iris* through it faster. One of his duties as master's mate was to supervise the hourly heaving of the log, and last time this had been done she was making eight knots. Her increased speed and the heavier sea meant more strain on her weakened side, and the pumps had not been stopped during Tom Evans's brief funeral; but the working-parties who manned them wrought with a will, because they knew she would raise the English coast sooner than had been expected.

'A moving ceremony, my friend.'

Mr Fitton, turning, was not best pleased to find Colonel Tate at his side. He had been aware of the colonel moving about the deck during the morning, chatting with the hands and apparently making himself generally agreeable, but had so far had no speech with him.

'Short,' Tate continued sententiously, 'but so is life itself, sir. And moving. I declare I shed a tear.'

With his black three-cornered hat set squarely on his grey-white hair, which was long enough to droop on the shoulders of his brown coat, he looked like a somewhat attenuated Quaker.

'I trust you've been comfortable aboard *Iris*, sir,' said Mr Fitton as politeness demanded.

'Remarkably so, sir, thankee. Captain Newnham has been most kind. If I didn't know you're all mighty anxious to get home I'd wish the voyage to be longer.'

Colonel Tate fell silent, and Mr Fitton felt obliged to keep the conversation going.

'It's not a great distance from France to England,' he said lamely.

The colonel turned the gaze of his large pale eyes upon him. 'That is so, sir,' he nodded. 'Some twenty miles at the north end of your Channel, as I believe. And that fact I find remarkable.'

'In what respect, may I ask?'

'Why, that two nations who've been at war for four years should still be kept apart by a strip of water no wider than Delaware Bay.'

'The Channel is our chief defence,' explained Mr Fitton patiently. 'While the Fleet commands it the French can't cross.'

'So I am aware, my friend, so I am aware. But the Channel can be crossed from north to south as well as from south to north.'

'You believe, then, that we should invade France? But our army is insufficient even for the defence of our overseas possessions. We couldn't hope to effect anything against the French by an invasion. If the Austrians were to make any progress –'

'Pardon me, sir, but the Austrians won't make a mite

of progress against General Carnot. Their tactics are outmoded. So, if you'll give me leave to say so, are those of the British Army. But I'm not disputing your opinion concerning an invasion.'

Colonel Tate leaned an elbow on the rail and visibly unlimbered his bony jaw. It was evident that he was about to launch himself on a favourite subject.

'The military science, sir,' he began ponderously, 'is one I have studied considerably for a good many years. I've been a soldier of fortune. I've fought against Redskins and Dagoes. I've fought against Hessians and British. I was at Brandywine with Washington and I've served under General Arnold – a fine tactician, sir. I recall an incident when I was with Arnold at the first Saratoga battle –'

The drawling voice went on, but Mr Fitton ceased to listen. He was not much interested in Colonel Tate's military career and there were more interesting things on the sea horizon. A long row of moving objects topped the dark bar ahead – the upper sails of a convoy heading down Channel; East Indiamen, probably. For *Iris* was entering the English sea-lanes, the busy avenues of trade with the Indies and the Americas. Some while ago Mr Collins had hailed the masthead lookout and told him to confine his reports to the sighting of land, for the sails of coasting vessels were coming into view every few minutes. The frigate could not be much more than ten miles from the coast now, he thought.

A word pronounced with emphasis by the colonel penetrated his abstraction.

'Terror,' Tate was saying weightily. 'The deadly weapon, as Benedict Arnold called it. Mighty effective if used as I've suggested. You agree, sir?'

'I'm afraid I don't follow you, colonel,' Mr Fitton said apologetically. 'My attention was distracted by the shipping yonder.'

'Then I will recapitulate,' said the colonel, unperturbed. 'Observe, sir, the coastline of France. Five hundred – six hundred miles of coastline, sir, as I calculate. A thousand bays and inlets and a fair sprinkling of them available for an enemy landing. Because why? Because the French can't in nature defend them all with forts and batteries and sentinels, sir. And the British Navy commands the approaches all the way round. Why in tarnation the British Navy hasn't grasped its opportunity beats me – beats me, sir.'

'If you mean the opportunity of raiding,' Mr Fitton said a trifle stiffly, 'it has been grasped on a good many –'

'A frigate lands a party and destroys a battery. What's the effect of that? The French build another battery twice the strength of t'other. It's no mere landing party, I'm advocating but a small army.'

'I thought we agreed that an invasion was –'

'It's plain you didn't attend to my exposition, my friend. Mark me, now.'

Colonel Tate faced his companion squarely, his skinny forefinger striking the palm of his other hand to emphasize his points. He spoke with a great deal more animation than Mr Fitton had hitherto heard him use.

'Firstly, the raid of terror – that's my name for it – is not aimed at the enemy's armed forces. It's aimed at the people, sir, the nation. Strike terror into the heart of the people, show 'em their defences are useless. Do that, and your war's half won. Secondly, the raid's not an invasion in the usual sense. A small force – a thousand men, maybe two thousand – is landed secretly, by night. They push inland, killing and burning as they go.' There was an unpleasant relish in the colonel's tone as he said this. 'And they'd find support from the discontented, the rebels against the ruling tyranny. There's the Breton royalists ready to rise again, sir.'

'Unless your raiding army had more support than that it would be cut off and eventually destroyed,' Mr Fitton objected.

Colonel Tate

'What of that, sir, what of that? The mischief would have been done. If I was to command such a force my men should be – what's a word for it? Expendable – that's it. Men to terrorize the country, men with licence to rape and murder and burn!' The colonel's excitement was growing. 'Redskin warfare! That's what's needed for a terror raid!'

'You'd not bring savages to fight in Europe?' Mr Fitton could not keep the disgust from his voice. 'The rules of warfare would surely –'

'Darn the rules of warfare! You want a victory over the French nation and you'll get it quickest if you use the deadliest weapons, sir!'

Tate's voice had risen and lost its drawl, and his long angular face was contorted into a ferocious grin. His pale eyes flickered and blinked, with a strange light in them. Mr Fitton began to think him mad.

'As for savages,' the colonel went on rapidly, 'I'd find 'em here in Europe, ready to hand. The jails, sir, and the condemned cells. There's the material for my terror expedition. I'd turn 'em loose, dress 'em in red uniforms head-to-foot, and call 'em the Red Devils. Or in black and call 'em the Black Legion. It'll all add to the terror. By the Eternal, I'd not refuse to lead 'em myself!'

'May I ask,' said Mr Fitton curiously, 'if you propose to submit this plan to some authority in London, colonel?'

The queer light faded from Colonel Tate's eyes. He cleared his throat noisily and replied, after a pause, in his customary drawl.

'That's as maybe, sir, that's as maybe.' He frowned suddenly. 'I'll thank you to keep the matter of my remarks to yourself.'

Before Mr Fitton could reply, Midshipman Fitzroy appeared at the colonel's elbow.

'Captain's compliments, sir,' piped Fitzroy, 'and he'd be obliged if you'd join him in the cabin.'

'Thankee, sonny,' said Colonel Tate. 'I'll come along.'

Without a further glance at the master's mate he stalked away across the deck, leaving Mr Fitton considerably puzzled. Tate's cool manner since he had been discovered in *Garonne*'s cabin contrasted oddly with the fierce enthusiasm with which he had outlined his fantastic plan for a terror raid. Mr Fitton had read accounts of the widespread sympathy among Americans for Britain's struggle against the Revolutionary Government in France and had considered these accounts over-optimistic; it was, after all, only fourteen years since the American colonists had won their own war against what they considered a despotic tyranny. He could concede, however, that there might be enthusiasts ready to journey across the Atlantic in order to aid what they had once called their mother country. But Colonel Tate did not strike him as being one of these. The man had called himself a soldier of fortune, and he seemed obsessed with his wildcat scheme for landing an army of jail-birds to terrorize a countryside. It had sounded almost as if he didn't care what countryside he terrorized. It was comforting to think that if he did indeed reach London and gain the ear of some authority in Whitehall or the Horse Guards his ridiculous plans would be peremptorily declined.

'Land ho! La-and ho!'

The screech from the masthead drove Colonel Tate and his peculiarities from Mr Fitton's thoughts. It was followed by an outburst of cheers and talk from the men on deck, quelled instantly by the first lieutenant's angry roar and a rapid succession of orders. All hands except the men at the pumps were turned-to in the preparations for arrival in port.

Iris, well ahead of her prize, closed the low green shores that rose slowly above a grey sea, and in the late afternoon of a mild winter's day brought Penlee Point on her larboard beam and entered the Sound. Drake's

Island with the clustered buildings of the port beyond, the higher ground above Plymouth Dock and its raw stonework, a 74 at moorings off Torpoint – Mr Fitton, in charge of successive working-parties below decks, saw nothing of these. By the time he came on deck, to find the frigate moored a cable-length from the *Pegasus* 74, Captain Newnham had gone ashore with his passenger.

In the days that followed Mr Fitton gave no thought to Colonel William Tate. He had other things to occupy him, and it was highly improbable that he would ever see the man again.

2 Winter Journey

1

Among the more recent buildings adjacent to the new township of Plymouth Dock was a stone frigate. This was the seamen's name for the naval barracks, a long two-storeyed building fronted with an elaborate portico and surrounded by a high-walled parade-ground whose single gateway was guarded by marine sentries. It was not unlike a prison, except that it was a good deal cleaner and its inmates had their liberty at prescribed times. This building, Mr Fitton discovered, was to be his home for an indeterminate period.

The fate of *Iris* and her prize had been decided two days after her arrival in harbour. The frigate, having had her shot-holes plugged, was to sail for her home port with the minimum of crew necessary to work her; the residue of her hands was to be divided, some to be transhipped to *Pegasus*, who was manning, and the rest ashore to the naval barracks to await drafting. *Garonne* would remain at Plymouth, where a prize court would assess her value. As *Pegasus* wanted no master's mates, Mr Fitton was ordered to pack his few belongings in his sea-chest and report to the duty officer at the barracks.

Resigned, as his philosophy required, to circumstances over which he had no control, he found life in barracks tolerable enough for the first few days. The stone frigate was run very much like a wooden ship of the line, except that her captain, who suffered from the gout, was never seen, and his elderly lieutenants were better acquainted with the social life of Plymouth than with seamanship. Watches were kept as at sea and Mr Fitton found himself supervising the cleaning of mess-decks and occasionally serving on night duty. He shared a small mess with three warrant officers and another master's mate; none of his messmates from *Iris* were in the barracks, though thirty of her seamen, including Sam Evans, made a majority in the lower-deck mess.

The talk at the mess-deck table was enlightening to a man who had been away from land so long. He learned for the first time of the British successes in the West Indies and of General Bonaparte's repeated victories over the Austrian armies in Italy; of the army's failure to establish a footing in French-ruled Holland. Discussions of Spain's entry into the war in October were mainly concerned with the extra chance of prize-money this afforded, a chance which (it was considered) no one in the barracks would be able to take. Rumour, well authenticated, said that *Pegasus* was the first of a small squadron that was being sent from Portsmouth to be stationed at Plymouth in case the French should send another armada to attack the West Country, and that they would all be drafted to one or other of these ships. Mr Fitton made an opportunity to ask Mr Caldecott, the most approachable of the elderly lieutenants, whether he knew when the additional vessels would arrive.

'It can hardly be less than a fortnight,' Caldecott told him good-naturedly. 'One 74 and a few small craft, I'm told. A dozen officers will be useful – they're always short of men at the balls here.'

Mr Fitton, after considering this information, decided to apply for a week's leave. He was entitled to it, and though he had no home to go to he could at least take the opportunity of being his own master for a few days.

He had drawn his back pay from the Pay Office and could afford to make a short journey that would show him something of this unfamiliar county of Devonshire. He made his application through the friendly Caldecott and was shortly afterwards summoned to the office of Lieutenant Dunn, a grizzled man who represented the absent captain.

'You must be mad,' Dunn grunted when Mr Fitton, questioned, explained his purpose. 'Traipsing the mud of this bloody shire in midwinter. However, you can have leave – six days. What's today's date?'

'Fifth of February, sir.'

'You'll report here by noon on the 12th. Leave as from end of the morning watch tomorrow.'

Thus presented with brief freedom, Mr Fitton was conscious of a mild excitement. He was country bred and as a boy had found adventure in wandering the lanes and wooded hills of Cheshire; perhaps he could recapture something of that youthful delight in journeying on foot. He had no map and little or no knowledge of the local topography. Should he start walking north from Plymouth and see where he came to? Better, maybe, to get clear of Plymouth by coach before taking to his feet; there were coaches, he knew, that ran to Tavistock and Launceston. His messmates, appraised at supper of his forthcoming leave, made ribald comments but offered no useful suggestions. His plans were still undecided at eight bells of the morning watch.

He was alone in the brick-walled cabin he shared with the other master's mate, packing his few necessaries into a stout canvas satchel that would serve him as a travelling valise. Pair of razors; clean shirt; *The Moral Discourses* of Epictetus in its worn calf binding; woollen muffler; money in a wash-leather bag. Boat-cloak – he would need to wear that for it was drizzling outside though mild and windless. The buckled shoes had seen better days but the soles were still thick enough to stand up to a day or two of walking –

A knock at the cabin door interrupted him and he opened it to find Sam Evans standing there. The big seaman's face wore a curiously sheepish expression.

'Well, Sam,' Mr Fitton said pleasantly, 'what can I do for you?'

In the course of his barracks duties he had several times exchanged brief greetings with Leading Seaman Evans. The fact that they were shipmates put ashore together seemed to warrant this more familiar address.

'If I might have a word, sir,' said Sam.

'Come in. I'm packing – going on leave.'

'I know, sir.' The seaman edged cautiously into the cabin and stood nervously fingering the hem of his canvas smock. 'I heard as you got six days leave. There's no leave for ratings, not outside the limits o' the port,' he added. ' 'Tis captain's orders.'

'I'm sorry about that. But I don't see that I can –'

'Nay, sir, regulations is regulations an' you can't go agin 'em. But – beggin' pardon, sir, but will you be goin' home or such?'

Mr Fitton shook his head. 'I've no home, and Cheshire's too far. I don't know yet where I'll go. I thought of making a journey –'

'A journey, by hooky!' Sam broke in, his blue eyes widening suddenly. 'Then –'

He stopped and massaged his thatch of iron-grey hair in manifest uncertainty.

'Out with it, Sam,' said Mr Fitton briskly.

'Aye aye, sir. 'Tis – well, if you remember, sir, consarnin' Tom, sayin' as how if there was something you could do –'

'Of course I remember. And you've thought of something?'

Sam fumbled in the breast of his smock and held out a small object. It was a highly coloured miniature of a man, head and shoulders, in a cheap gilt frame. His words came in a rush.

'Tom had it done in Portsmouth. He allus said he'd like Gwennie to have it if aught happened to him. I'd thought to take it to her meself, but seems I'm hard aground here. I wondered if maybe you'd –'

'Of course I'll take it. Tom was this Gwennie's sweetheart?'

'Aye, sir – red-haired gal, Gwennie Jones.'

'Where does Miss Jones live? Portsmouth?'

Sam hesitated for a long moment. 'Pembrokeshire, seven mile south o' Fishguard.'

'Pembrokeshire!' Mr Fitton repeated in some dismay. 'Sam, I've only six days leave and I doubt if I can get any extension.'

'You'd do it easy in six days, sir,' Sam said quickly. 'That's if you don't mind spendin' a sovereign or two. I've got me pay,' he added, 'and I'll stand –'

'No you won't. You say I can get there and back in six days. How do I shape my course?'

'Same as Tom did two year ago when he got put ashore here. The coach for Launceston –'

Mr Fitton listened attentively to his proposed itinerary. The Launceston coach would take him on as far as Holsworthy on the first day. With a hired nag and an early start he could do the seventeen miles to Bideford in a morning. There were a lot of vessels sailing between Bideford and Milford Haven, day and night, and with luck he'd get a passage across the Bristol Channel with little delay – a twelve hour passage with any reasonable wind, it was. Then it would be coach or horseback for the last fourteen miles.

'That'd be the third day out, sir,' Sam ended triumphantly. 'Gives you three for comin' back.'

It seemed to Mr Fitton that this optimistic timetable relied heavily on chance, and that he was very likely to overstay his leave; but the prospect of extending his journey into Wales was an attractive one and its object satisfied his wishes. A second's hesitation and his decision was made.

'Very well. Tell me how I'm to find Miss Jones's home. And look sharp about it, Sam – I've to cross the Torpoint ferry and the coach leaves at four bells.'

'Aye aye, sir.' Sam's face lost its delighted grin and became serious. ' 'Tain't her home, sir. Gwennie's in service with a French lady, Madame de Callac's her name. One o' these Emmy Grays, as they call 'em, escaped from them murderin' Frogs. She leased Long Warren – that's the name o' the house – from Colonel Knox two year ago. You'll easy find Long Warren. Land at Milford an' go seven mile north to Haverfordwest. 'Nother seven mile north to a place they call Wolf's Castle. Hard a-starb'd there on a quarter-mile o' lane, look out for a biggish house on your larboard hand, an' that's Long Warren.'

'That seems clear enough.' Mr Fitton wrapped the miniature in his woollen muffler and put it in the satchel. 'I'll break the news to Gwennie as gently as I can, Sam.'

'Thankee, sir. An' there's one thing more. Will Devonald's brig *Olwen* might be at Bideford. Will's an old friend of mine an' plies regular between Milford an' Bideford – 'cept when he's away pickin' up a cargo farther south. That's atween you an' me,' Sam added quickly.

'I'm not a revenue officer.' Mr Fitton slung his satchel on his shoulder. 'It's my opinion that any man who can bring brandy from France in wartime is doing a service to his country.'

'There's a many o' the gentry in Pembrokeshire thinks same as you, sir. Anyways, if Will's brig should be in Bideford an' you tells him you're takin' a message for Sam Evans, he'll put you across, an' he won't want passage money.'

'Devonald. I'll ask for him,' said Mr Fitton; he put on his hat and flung the boat-cloak round his shoulders. 'Have you any message for Miss Gwennie?'

'P'raps you'd tell her I'm thinkin' of her, sir.' Sam hesitated and then held out his hand. 'Good luck – an' thankee again.'

Mr Fitton came out of the barracks gate, past the perfunctory salute of the marine sentry, and strode rapidly along the dingy street towards the Torpoint ferry. The street was a succession of muddy puddles, the steady drizzle was heavy enough to penetrate his cloak. He found it hard to recapture that youthful exhilaration in setting forth on a journey. An hour later he was finding it harder still.

There were few people travelling and he had got his place on the coach without trouble. It was an 'outside', and he sat muffled in his wet boat-cloak on the box, on the windward side of the equally muffled coachman. When they had climbed the hill behind Plymouth, the rain, with an east wind behind it, swept down from the heights of Dartmoor in cold relentless torrents. Mr Fitton did his best to enjoy a jolting progress very different from the swoop and roll of a ship; but he could not help reflecting that he had been less uncomfortable than this at sea.

2

The carrier's cart discharged a more cheerful Mr Fitton in the middle of Bideford town a little after noon on the second day of his journey. The little inn at Holsworthy was responsible for this cheerfulness; they had dried his wet things, fed him plainly but plentifully, and found him a carrier's cart that started at eight in the morning for Bideford.

The road was a poor one, very roughly metalled and

hilly, and the carrier's nag had taken four hours to haul them the seventeen miles. But the rain had stopped, and Mr Fitton, gazing about him from his seat beside the silent driver, had found interest in travelling through a countryside new to him, bare and barren though it was. When they came down through the leafless oakwoods below Littleham and saw the white houses of Bideford town clustered at the tip of the Torridge estuary, with the grey waters of the Bristol Channel spreading beyond, he felt the satisfaction of a traveller who has crossed a county from one sea to another.

Bideford's long quay was busy and thronged with shipping, fishing-boats and small brigs and a schooner or two, some of them loading or discharging cargo. Out in the stream, where the tide was low but beginning to make, half a dozen larger vessels lay at moorings. Every third house of the many that stood fronting onto the quay seemed to be a tavern, and he turned into the first that he came to. The long low-beamed room was full of tobacco smoke and the buzz of talk from the score or so of leathery-faced men who sat at small tables with pewter tankards in front of them. He made his way to the bar, ordered a pint of ale and bread-and-cheese, and put his question to the bearded landlord.

'*Olwen?*' the landlord repeated, and raised his voice. 'Hey, boys! Be Will Devonald in port?'

'Nay,' someone called in reply. 'He'm to the Haven – sailed morning tide yesterday.'

'Be you a friend of Will's, sir?' inquired the landlord, setting a brimming tankard on the counter.

'We've never met. I thought to take passage to Milford Haven in *Olwen* if Devonald was bound there. My luck's not in.'

Mr Fitton took his bread-and-cheese and ale to a table near the window and sat munching reflectively. It had of course been a very long chance that his arrival at

Bideford should coincide neatly with *Olwen*'s sailing, but there was still a possibility that another vessel might be making the passage while this easterly wind was fair for it. If he had to wait for two days his leave would expire before he could get back to Plymouth. The leisurely journey he had promised himself, he perceived, had become a race with time and circumstance.

'By'r leave, master.' A stocky black-haired man had come to stand at his table. 'Was ee seeking to cross to Milford?'

Mr Fitton looked up quickly. 'I was and am. Are you sailing?'

'Iss. Tonight's tide. I can give ee passage. Studley, brig *Cormorant*.'

'My name's Fitton and I'll be glad to sail with you, Captain Studley. What time do you cast off?'

'Meet you here at sundown and see you aboard. What's it worth to you, Mr Fitton?'

Mr Fitton grinned. 'It's worth the least you can bring yourself to charge me, captain.'

'Guinea suit you?'

'You're too modest, captain. Done with you.'

Studley unsmiling as ever, shook hands on the bargain and returned to his table and tankard. Mr Fitton finished his frugal meal with increased satisfaction. So prompt a furnishing of his need seemed to show that this journey had the approval of his Tutelary Genius, a Stoic conception which he was inclined to believe in. He spent the few remaining hours of a cloudy afternoon strolling about the port, returning to the tavern for an early supper. Studley duly arrived to escort him along the quay and on board *Cormorant*. From his curt answers to Mr Fitton's questions it appeared that if the easterly held steady they might raise the Pembrokeshire coast at first light.

Cormorant was as small a two-master as any Mr Fitton had seen. Studley led the way down a ladder aft and pushed open the door of a small stern-cabin.

'Mate's cabin,' he said. 'You'll find blankets on the berth.'

'But your mate will –'

Studley grunted. 'Don't carry a mate, master. Sail mun wi' four men and a boy.'

This minimal crew showed itself adequate as *Cormorant*, with accustomed ease, slipped down the four miles of estuary and out into the dark of the open sea beyond the bar. The sea was slight, the east wind steady. Mr Fitton stayed on deck for a while, wrapped in his boat-cloak against the keen wind. Then it occurred to him that on this short voyage he had the rare opportunity of spending the whole night in his bunk, and he went below. The dark little cabin smelt of Stockholm tar but the blankets were dry and warm. With the familiar sounds of a ship under way in his ears he slept a good deal more soundly than he had done in the naval barracks and didn't wake until dawn. Studley was at the helm when he came on deck in the half-light.

'Linney Head,' he called, pointing for'ard.

Ahead to starboard the coast of Wales showed a thin black line on the barely visible horizon. *Cormorant*, though courses and topsails were all the canvas on her stumpy masts, was making seven or eight knots with a keen easterly wind just abaft the beam, and as daylight grew slowly across the furrowed water so the coast rose and spread, closing in on either hand as she brought St Ann's Head abeam to larboard. By sunrise of a cold but clear morning, the brig's four hands had brailed up her courses and she was gliding in past an outgoing fleet of fishing-boats towards the quays of Milford port.

Mr Fitton, with a mugful of scalding coffee (brought by the ship's boy) inside him, surveyed his approaching landing-place with some disappointment. He had pictured Wales as a mountainous country, but there was nothing mountainous or romantic about this north coast of Milford Haven. Low hills, drab and treeless, flanked the buildings of a port which even a gleam of wintry sunshine could not beautify. But it was a busy port, with the masts of many craft clustered along its quays like a thicket and on the quays themselves the movement of men and carts. A grey church tower rose among the houses of the little town, and looking beyond and above it he could see a ribbon of road mounting across the brown slope of a hill. That would be his road to Haverfordwest seven miles away.

The taking-in of topsails and jib was followed by an outburst of objurgatory shouting. Captain Studley, it appeared, was accustomed to berth his little ship at a particular spot and an intrusive dory had tied up there. The dory was hastily hauled away; fenders were slung outboard, ropes sailed across the rail and were made fast; *Cormorant* was brought to lie snugly alongside with a dexterity that roused Mr Fitton's admiration.

'Thank you, captain,' he said as he handed over his passage-money. 'A fast passage and a comfortable one. When do you sail for Bideford again?'

His hopes were quickly dispelled. *Cormorant* was here to wait for a cargo from Pembroke. Might be three days or four.

'*Olwen* might be sailing sooner,' Studley added.

'She's here?'

'Iss. Alongside half-a-cable west on the quay. You'll likely find Will Devonald on board.'

Mr Fitton shook hands and stepped ashore in Wales. It was not much different from England, he told himself as he made his way along the quay past rumbling wagons and piled crates. When he heard two angry stevedores swearing at each other in what was undoubtedly a foreign language he was reassured; it restored the pleasant persuasion that he had journeyed from one country to another.

The brig *Olwen*, when he found her, proved to be a vessel of considerably greater tonnage than *Cormorant*.

She was taking in cargo, and he dodged through a procession of men carrying barrels and boxes to scramble aboard. A man who was directing the stowage told him the cap'n was below in the after cabin, and when he had descended a ladder and ducked in through an open door he found Captain Devonald at breakfast. His attempt at apology was cut short.

'Never mind that, man. Have you breakfasted? Come you in and join me – I'm always glad o' company.'

Will Devonald was a big man with a round humorous face and an untidy thatch of grey hair. He listened to the brief explanation Mr Fitton thought it necessary to give before sitting down, and then, half-rising from his chair, extended a horny hand.

'You're doubly welcome, man. I've had no news o' Sam Evans these three months.' He pushed a knife and a platter across the table. 'Bread and beef and small ale – help yourself and let's have the whole story.'

He heard the tale of Mr Fitton's present mission and its inception without interrupting and then shook his head sadly.

'So Tom's gone. Well, there's nothing sure in life but death. And you're off to break the news to Gwennie at Long Warren?'

'I don't look forward to that, I assure you,' Mr Fitton said with sincerity.

Devonald pursed his lips. 'I doubt whether it'll break Gwennie Jones's heart. Tom was rare sweet on her, but she's a flighty piece and being in service with a French noblewoman hasn't sobered her.' He chuckled. 'You'll be calling on a good customer of mine at Long Warren.'

'You mean the French lady – Madame de Callac?'

'Aye. A rare one for looking after her belly, she is.' The captain shot a keen glance at his guest. 'Maybe Sam told you I sometimes make a voyage south of Scilly?'

Mr Fitton grinned. 'To where there's right Bordeaux to be had in casks? You needn't fear I'll pass that on to the gaugers, captain.'

'I wouldn't think so low of you, sir,' Devonald said primly. 'But it's not only a cask of Bordeaux I bring across now and then for Long Warren — it's Périgord truffles and Callac pigeons. Pigeon pie and truffles, she says to me once, I must have, and there's no pigeons that eat so well as the Callac pigeons.'

'Someone must go to some trouble to get them for her,' Mr Fitton commented. 'Before you take them on board, I mean.'

'Aye. — Fill your mug, man. — Madame and her husband the Comte had this big estate o' Callac, seemingly, before he had his head taken off and she escaped across Channel. The folk o' Callac keep a kindness for her — there's a mort o' Royalists in Brittany — and get the goods to Roscoff where I picks 'em up. That's what she told me.' Devonald paused, his round face suddenly serious. 'It don't seem fair, all the same, she with her pigeon pies and such and the folk here short of food. Bread's ten times the price it was last year. There was riots over it in Pembroke five weeks ago — militia called out and all. And if you'd passed through Haverfordwest market-square yesterday you'd have seen a man in the pillory there — aye, punished for writing and printing verses against King George.'

'If this was France it would have been the guillotine for him, not the pillory,' said Mr Fitton, setting down his empty mug. 'A few malcontents can't hurt us, captain. But you remind me that I've now to find my way to Haverfordwest and I mustn't linger. As I told you, I've but the six days —'

'Never fret yourself, man,' Captain Devonald broke in heartily. '*Duw*! I've plotted your course for you while we was talking. Listen here, now.'

It was no empty boast. The two wagons that had brought part of *Olwen*'s cargo down from Haverfordwest would be starting back in half an hour and Mr

Fitton could take a lift in one of 'em, right to the market-square in the town. Morris's livery stable was next door to the Cawdor Arms in the High Street and if he wanted a nag Morris would hire him a sound one – mention Will Devonald's name and he wouldn't be unduly robbed. Same with Williams of the Cawdor Arms, where Mr Fitton had better put up when he got back from Long Warren. And then, if he could get himself down to Milford quay by nine of the clock next morning – not later, for the tide wouldn't wait – he could have a passage to Bideford in *Olwen*.

For this solution of his travel problems Mr Fitton was sincerely grateful, and said so.

'But it seemed to me, captain,' he added, frowning, 'that you were getting ready to sail this morning.'

'What's a day's delay?' Devonald clapped him on the shoulder. 'You're a shipmate o' Sam Evans, man.'

So it came about that an hour before noon on the third day of his journey Mr Fitton left Haverfordwest's cobbled streets behind him and took the road northward. And he took it on foot. He had originally planned to use his leave for a pedestrian tour, and the only walking he had done so far was from one conveyance to another.

It was market-day in Haverfordwest and the little town had been crowded with chattering Welsh women, nearly all of them wearing their characteristic dress of bright red shawl, tall black hat, and spotless white *brat* or apron. Looking back as he left the market-square, Mr Fitton was struck by its resemblance to a military parade-ground full of soldiers. But towns and throngs, however picturesque, were not his present interest. He had seven hours of daylight before him, and he would cover the fourteen miles to Long Warren and back on Shanks's Mare.

3

It was a good day for fast walking. The grey February sky opened now and then to let through a gleam of sun, and though the wind still blew from the east there was no need to get the boat-cloak out of his satchel. The road, narrow and roughly metalled, held at first to a low ridge that afforded glimpses of a river valley on his left and wider views over the rolling countryside on his other hand, a countryside sparsely inhabited but populous with cattle and sheep. In his first mile he met two pony-carts and three wagons, but after that he saw no one except a shepherd on a hill pasture above him. He swung along at a steady stride, and when the road dropped into a wooded glen at noon by his watch he was absurdly pleased to learn, from a milestone, that he had come four miles from Haverfordwest in one hour.

A stone bridge crossed the river here, and on its mossy parapet Mr Fitton spread his cloak to sit and munch a currant bun he had bought in Haverfordwest market-square. He was enjoying himself. This little journey could hardly be called adventurous but it was as different as could be from life aboard ship. And for the next half-hour the road conformed more closely to his preconceived idea of Welsh scenery. It wound up a deep valley narrow enough to be called a gorge, with the river foaming on his right hand, passing below steep woodlands where the leafless trees revealed the slopes of grey boulders. At the upper end of the gorge the hillside on his left was crowned with a bristle of weird crags, and a mile farther on he came to a cluster of stone cottages lying a little off the road. A man toiling with a mattock in the stony field before the cottages answered his shouted query with a nod and a volley of Welsh. The nod at least assured him that this was Wolf's Castle, and the grassy mound of a Norman motte beside the road confirmed it. *Hard a-starb'd there on a quarter-mile o' lane* – Sam's direction would have been easier to follow had there been a lane. But a step or two past the motte revealed the lane, a mere track but recently metalled, running level across undulating fields on the right. A hundred paces along it he came in sight of a white house in a fold of the hillside on the left of the track. This must be Long Warren.

The house was not a large one and looked like a cross between a farmhouse and a gentleman's residence. A moving ray of sunshine passed over it as he approached, lighting the two or three stone outbuildings that rose above the tall evergreens that flanked the house. Mr Fitton pushed open a six-barred wooden gate and advanced up a short gravelled drive. On his right, through an opening in the bushes, he glimpsed a screen of what looked like fishing-net, and beyond it a squat stone tower with a row of apertures near its top; a monotonous *coo-roo-coo* reminded him of the Comtesse de Callac's pigeon pies and removed any doubt that he had reached his destination. He was making for the wide gabled porch when he saw a chaise standing in the stable-yard to his left and a lean grey-haired man with broom and bucket washing its wheels. He crossed to the man, gave him good afternoon, and inquired whether this was Long Warren.

'That is the name of the house.' The man's glance travelled from the visitor's muddy shoes to his face. 'Sir,' he added.

He spoke with a marked foreign accent and his stare held a hint of suspicion. A Frenchman who had followed his mistress into exile, Mr Fitton decided.

'I'm the bearer of a message to a young woman in service here,' he said, 'Miss Gwennie Jones. If you'd tell her there's a man from Plymouth –'

'*Qui est-ce, Gaston?*'

The voice that interrupted him was singularly clear and musical. Turning, he saw that a woman was coming towards them from the direction of the pigeon-loft, a small woman in a blue-grey gown trimmed with fur. She was hatless, her dark hair plainly dressed, and carried an empty basket under her arm, but her bearing as she approached and stood regarding him was that of a queen. Mr Fitton doffed his hat and made his best bow.

'Have I the honour of addressing Madame de Callac?' he said, straightening himself.

'I am Simone de Callac, sir.' Her English had only the slightest accent. 'And your name, please?'

The eyes that were calmly surveying him were precisely the colour of her gown, he noted, and they were set in a face which – though hardly to be called beautiful – was charmingly expressive. At this moment it was expressing slight annoyance, and he was suddenly aware that he was staring rudely.

'Michael Fitton, madame,' he said hastily, 'at your service. I'm here with a message for Miss Jones.'

'For Gwennie?' The blue-grey eyes glanced quickly from the canvas satchel to its owner's square-jawed brown face. 'You have come far?'

'From Plymouth. Today from Haverfordwest.'

'On foot?'

He smiled at the incredulity in her tone. 'Only these last seven miles, madame.'

'You must take some refreshment.' She hesitated a moment, then handed her basket to the man Gaston and turned away. 'Come. We will find Gwennie for you.'

'I fear I bring bad news for Gwennie,' Mr Fitton said as they walked together towards the porch.

'One of her family is ill, or dead, perhaps?'

'No, madame – her sweetheart. He is dead.'

She turned a puzzled face to him. 'Sweetheart? What is that?'

'*Son amoureux*, madame,' he told her.

'*Vous parlez ma langue, alors!*' she exclaimed delightedly.

'*Très indifféremment, je vous assure.* Your English, madame,' he added, 'is more fluent than my French.'

'I have been for two years in your country.' The Comtesse led the way into the house as she spoke. '*Mais* – the poor Gwennie! She will be *désolée*. – Seat yourself, Mr Fitton, and I will ring for her.'

They had entered an oak-raftered room on one side of the hallway. A big dresser laden with ranged plates and dishes occupied most of one wall and a log smouldered in the wide stone fireplace. Mr Fitton obediently sat down in one of the two chairs near the fire and took the miniature of Tom Evans from his satchel. Madame de Callac picked up a little bell from a table near the door and rang it loudly.

'You will tell her as gently as you can, will you not?' she said. 'She is a good girl, though perhaps a little – *volage*.'

'I'll do my best, madame,' Mr Fitton said doubtfully, 'but it's a task I've never undertaken before.'

'Then I will speak to her first, if you will allow me. If this news is –'

She stopped speaking as a pretty red-haired girl in apron and frilled cap entered the room and dropped a curtsey.

'Gwennie –' the Comtesse took both her hands – 'this gentleman comes from Plymouth with a message for you. You must prepare yourself, *chérie*, to hear bad news, very bad news.'

She stepped back as Mr Fitton, miniature in hand, came forward. Gwennie, round-eyed and open-mouthed, faced him apprehensively.

'I'm a shipmate of Sam Evans, Miss Jones,' he said. 'Sam would have come himself if he was able to, and I was to tell you that he's thinking of you. He says that Tom wanted you to have this if anything happened to him.'

He held out the miniature. The girl received it from him without taking her eyes from his face.

'Tom?' she whispered.

Mr Fitton nodded. 'There was a fight at sea. Tom died fighting bravely against the French.'

For a moment Gwennie stood motionless, the miniature gripped tightly in her hand. Then she burst into tears, turned, and fled from the room.

'*Excusez!*' said the Comtesse quickly, and went out after her.

Mr Fitton went to the fireplace and stood looking down at the red glow. He felt as if a load had been lifted from his back. He was sorry for Gwennie, but remembering Will Devonald's comment that she was 'a flighty piece' and Madame de Callac's use of the word *volage* (which he took to mean 'fickle') he could hope that her grief wouldn't last for long. He turned as the Comtesse re-entered the room.

'I have sent Sarah, my cook, to Gwennie,' she said as she came towards him. 'She is Welsh and will give more comfort than I can. I think we could not have managed that sad business better than we did, Mr Fitton. And I think – no, I am sure – that I, as well as yourself, deserve a glass of wine.'

She brought a small wooden table to place between the two fireside chairs, then stood on tiptoe to reach a bottle and two glasses from a wall-cupboard. Mr Fitton, watching her, thought he had never seen anyone move so gracefully; and dismissed a momentary suspicion that it was a studied gracefulness.

'Madame is too kind,' he said politely.

'I shall require a return for my kindness.' She was filling the glasses as she spoke. 'You will sit in that chair, and I shall sit here, and you will tell me about the fight at sea and how poor Tom Evans was killed.'

Mr Fitton had no objection to obeying this behest. While he was giving his brief account of the encounter between *Iris* and *Garonne* a part of his mind was recalling amusedly the vicissitudes of his journey: the carrier's cart, Captain Studley's brig, the currant bun on the river-bridge, and now wine by the fireside with a lady of the French *noblesse*. The wine was a good claret, and he wondered whether it had come over with Will Devonald. At least it helped to loosen a tongue he was not much given to using, and he was ready to comply with Madame de Callac's demand for a description of his travels. The telling of the sea-fight had brought the enigmatic Colonel Tate to his mind for the first time in several days; but he thought it unnecessary to bring the colonel into his story.

'So, then, you are an officer of the Navy,' the Comtesse said when he had finished.

'I hold no commission, madame,' he told her. 'I'm rated master's mate – a tolerably humble rank in a ship.'

'And yet –' she hesitated – 'I think you are a man of birth?'

Mr Fitton was surprised and somewhat discomposed. 'I come of one of the oldest families in Britain,' he said shortly.

She nodded complacently. 'So I had thought. *Vous avez l'air*. Mine is also a very old family.' She sighed. '*Hélas*! In my poor country the day of the great families is over and the *canaille* have taken their place. The Château Callac, I am told, is falling into ruin. I am almost thankful that my husband is not alive to see the end of the nobility of France.'

Mr Fitton, who had little faith in the theories of blue blood, steered the conversation on a divergent course.

'You have my deepest sympathy, madame,' he said. 'But – if you'll permit me to say so – you've chosen a lonely dwelling-place for your enforced exile.'

'*Pas du tout*!' she said quickly. 'I am not at all lonely, sir. Consider. I have my groom Gaston and my maid Sophie with me, I have a chaise and a horse. And my neighbours are nice friendly people.' She numbered them on slim fingers. 'There is Colonel Knox at

Minwere Lodge and Mrs Harries at Tregwynt, the Honourable Mr Thomas and young Mr Edwards with his pretty wife – all are within a chaise drive of Long Warren. Lord Cawdor's house is farther away, and yet I have been to a ball at Stackpole Court.' She flashed a smile at him. 'I find the British a most hospitable people.'

'I'm glad of that, madame, for your sake.'

'*Tout de même*, I have my fears,' she went on, suddenly serious. 'Continually I hear tales and rumours of disorder, in these parts and elsewhere – of riots and gatherings of protest against the Government. I read in the *Morning Chronicle* of republican societies and Levellers – one would say there are many in your country ready to rise and support the monsters who have ruined my country.'

Mr Fitton made to speak but was checked by her imperious gesture. The blue-grey eyes were fixed earnestly on him and the Comtesse's clear voice took on a more urgent note as she continued.

'Here in Wales, too, there is a stir of rebellion – Gaston, who has visited the taverns, tells me this. Welshmen say that theirs is a country separated from England by its different language and different customs. They seek independence, to rise and throw off the English yoke. I cannot but think, sir, that if the Jacobin ruffians in Paris were to launch an invasion –'

'Stop there, madame.'

Mr Fitton had been content to sip his wine and listen, watching the flicker of firelight on her face; he felt himself in a state of enchantment and wished it to continue. But now he roused himself and spoke at a length unusual with him.

'Forgive me, madame, but your fears are groundless. In France, I know, men aren't permitted to voice their discontents. In England we speak our grumbles freely and if they're loud enough the Government may take notice – if it doesn't it could be thrown out. But no one would think of replacing it with a Directory and a guillotine. As for the Welsh, they've wanted their independence for centuries, and I daresay some of them would show their teeth if they had another Owen Glendower to lead them. But mark my words, madame.' He set down his empty wine-glass and leaned forward. 'If ever this island was invaded by a French army there's not a man – Welsh or Scottish or English – who wouldn't fight tooth and nail to drive it into the sea.' He sat back, somewhat abashed by his own eloquence. 'That's about as likely as nuts in May,' he added more lightly. 'While the Navy commands the seas there can be no invasion.'

The Comtesse had seemed to listen intently to his words, frowning slightly. Now the frown vanished and she drank the last of her wine.

'What you have said has greatly reassured me, Mr Fitton,' she said with a smile at him. 'I shall sleep more comfortably tonight.'

The room had darkened noticeably since they had entered it; Mr Fitton was suddenly aware that this was a short February day and that he had a two-hour walk before him.

'And if I'm to sleep comfortably tonight,' he said, getting up, 'I must be on my way, madame.'

Madame de Callac rose to her feet. 'To Haverfordwest? But not on foot – Gaston shall put the horse to the chaise. It will take but a moment.'

'No, madame, by your leave. I much prefer to walk.'

'You will have walked fourteen miles today.'

'Fourteen paces is about as much as I'm able to walk aboard ship.' He collected hat and satchel and turned to face her. '*Madame, mes meilleurs remerciements pour votre hospitalité la plus charmante.*'

'*Monsieur, c'était à moi un grand plaisir.*'

She curtsied gracefully in response to his own bow, then led the way to the door.

'I shall do what I can to comfort the poor Gwennie,' she said as he shouldered his satchel in the porch.

'I'm sure of that, madame.'

She held out her hand. Mr Fitton took it and, after a second's hesitation, kissed it. The Comtesse didn't seem displeased.

'*Bon voyage, monsieur,*' she said.

'*Adieu, madame.*'

When he had gone as far as the gate he looked back, but she had re-entered the house.

After the warmth of the Long Warren fireside the darkening afternoon was chilly, and low grey clouds hid a sun which was near its setting. As he reached the road at Wolf's Castle, however, he retained within him a warmth that was not wholly attributable to one glass of claret. Simone de Callac lingered obsessively in his thoughts.

Anything unphilosophical or unreasonable in himself always interested Mr Fitton, and while he was swinging down the road into the twilight of the tree-clad gorge he was considering his unusual state of mind. Love at first sight was a foolery for callow youngsters and it was certainly not that. Some charm she had caught him with, however; perhaps it was her candid friendliness, or the grace of all her movements. Or the charm of her figure in its blue-grey dress, slim as a young girl's despite the fact that she must be nearing thirty. Perhaps it was simply that she was a woman. After all, she was the first lady he had spoken with for more than twelve months.

By the time he had reached the bridge where he had eaten his currant bun, he had decided that the last of these reasons accounted for everything. He would never see Madame de Callac again and she could be dismissed from his thoughts. Nevertheless, when he was passing the first lamplit cottages of Haverfordwest an hour later he was still thinking of that fireside interlude in the Long Warren parlour.

4

If Mr Fitton's Tutelary Genius had seemed to smile on his outward journey it was certainly not so with his return. He duly boarded Will Devonald's brig at Milford next morning and was warmly welcomed by the genial smuggler, but the wind had shifted to the south-east and risen to blow half-a-gale, a head wind for *Olwen*'s course once she had cleared the Haven. It was past noon of the following day before the brig had berthed at the Bideford quay, and no conveyance, nor even a horse, could be found for the seventeen miles to Holsworthy. The carrier's cart that took him to Holsworthy next day started late and had to call first at Torrington, so that it was dusk when he reached the little inn where he had spent the first night of his leave. The morning of 10 February saw him starting out on the only horse Holsworthy could provide, a miserable nag that cast a shoe two miles short of Launceston and had to be left there. Mr Fitton was now twenty-seven miles short of his destination and he had missed the coach from Launceston, but his blood was up; for to him it was a point of honour to report for duty before his leave expired. He walked the thirteen miles to Tavistock in four hours on a cold but rainless afternoon, left the inn at Tavistock in the back of a wagon going as far as Yelverton, and took to his feet again for a final nine miles of hilly road beset by rain squalls. At precisely five minutes before noon on the 12th he was shaking the drops from his wet boat-cloak outside Lieutenant Dunn's office-room.

'By God, you cut it damned fine, Mr Fitton!' Dunn said as he presented himself. 'The captain's sent round twice to know if you've returned. You're drafted. Your ship sails tomorrow so you'd best collect your traps and get on board without an instant's delay. *Curlew*, 12-gun cutter, at the arsenal quay.'

'Aye aye, sir. By your leave, sir, I must get a message to a seaman, Evans, before I go.'

'Well, you'd better look sharp – wait.' Dunn reached for a ledger, found a page, and ran his finger down a list. 'Draft for *Curlew*. M Fitton master's mate, B Kenyon seaman, S Evans seaman.' He looked up. 'You'll find your man on board.'

'Thank you, sir. And the captain's name?'

'She's a lieutenant's command and you're welcome to him.' Dunn permitted himself a grin. 'Grand-nephew of Lord Howe and calls himself the Honourable Beaufort Barrington.'

3   Secret Emissary

1

The afternoon was as dark and squally as the morning had been but to Mr Fitton it seemed a good deal brighter. As he walked quickly along the puddled road, a lad trundling his sea-chest on a barrow behind him, he considered his new drafting and decided that his Tutelary Genius was once again regarding him with favour.

Lieutenant the Honourable Beaufort Barrington had been a gawky junior midshipman in *Vestal*, with Mr Fitton as his senior in the 74's gunroom. Since that long-ago day their fortunes had been very different; Barrington, a younger son of Lord Talbot and related to the admiral commanding the Channel Fleet, had achieved his promotion, while Fitton – largely because of his tendency to act without orders – had risen no further than master's mate. The last time he had encountered Bony Barrington, he recalled, had been in Portsmouth Harbour, where Barrington had command of the duty cutter; it was a little surprising that Bony had not by now been given command of a brig-sloop or a gun-brig, with the epaulette of Master and Commander on his left shoulder.

The newly built arsenal quay was on the Plymouth Dock side of the harbour so he didn't have to cross on the ferry. It was a long quay, with many craft lying alongside, and he walked with his eye open for a tall single mast. A 12-gun cutter, as he knew though he had never served in one, was built and rigged for speed and was used for patrol duties and the carrying of dispatches; service in such a craft was unlikely to result in the acquisition of prize-money. But life on board would be less formal than in a frigate or ship of the line, and though he had adjudged Bony Barrington to be incorrigibly feather-brained he had always had a liking for him. *Curlew* would carry a crew of forty or fifty, with three warrant officers and a junior lieutenant under Barrington. Her guns –

His reflections came to an end as the cutter came in sight beyond a large brig taking in cargo. Her long flush-decked hull was shifting gently against the fenders slung between it and the quay wall, and the six closed gunports spaced along her rail glistened black in the rain. Half-a-dozen hands were coiling a rope up for'ard, and a single big figure in a tarpaulin coat stood by the shrouds amidships. To this seaman Mr Fitton, coming to a halt, addressed himself.

'Fitton, master's mate. Orders to join *Curlew*.'

In the moment of speaking he recognized Sam Evans, whose craggy face broke into a beaming smile.

'Come aboard, sir, if you please,' said Evans.

Mr Fitton climbed over the rail and touched his hat to the non-existent quarterdeck.

'I delivered your message, Sam,' he said quickly in an undertone.

'Thankee, sir.' Sam was hoisting the sea-chest inboard. 'How'd Gwennie take it?'

'She was upset, of course, but I think she'll get over it.' He tossed a shilling to the lad with the barrow. 'So we're to be shipmates –'

'Fitton!' shouted a high tenor voice, and he turned to see Lieutenant Barrington striding towards him.

'By God, I'm glad to –' Barrington stopped and

cleared his throat loudly. 'Welcome aboard, Mr Fitton,' he resumed with exaggerated formality. 'I am happy to have you with us.'

Mr Fitton touched his hat and grasped the hand his new captain extended to him. Bony, he was thinking, had hardly changed since *Vestal*'s gunroom – the same tall thin body, the same beaky nose and perpetually arched brows.

'Rees! Callaghan!' Barrington shouted. 'Mr Fitton's sea-chest to the after cabin larboard side. – Come with me,' he added, turning aft. 'I'll show you your quarters.'

Curlew's main cabin was a tiny place, though it ran the whole width of the cutter's stern, and Barrington had to stoop low as he led the way into it. He gestured Mr Fitton to one of the narrow locker-seats and sat down himself with a loud *whoosh*! of relief.

'Gad's me life!' he said feelingly. 'You're a sight for sore eyes, Fitton. I've been huntin' you up and down Channel. Run you to earth here and I'm told you're out and away and the scent's cold.'

'My leave expired only at noon today, sir.'

'I know, I know – but a feller can overstay his leave, y'know.' Barrington wagged his head deprecatingly. 'I did myself. It's why I've got *Curlew* instead of the *Alceste* ship-sloop, so the vice-admiral told me. I was up at Meriton's place for the shootin' – and by God, Fitton, I was showin' top form! Mind you, my gun had a deal to do with it. That's it up there.' He pointed to a long sporting-gun hanging on the bulkhead. 'The very latest from Joe Copley in the Strand. The lock's a beauty – I'll show you.'

'You said you were hunting me, sir,' Mr Fitton said quickly as he began to rise.

Barrington sat down again. 'So I was, by God! *Iris* came into Portsmouth the day I got *Curlew*'s orders – you were in *Iris* accordin' to the last news I had of you – and I moved heaven and earth and the port captain to get you drafted to me. Then I find you've been left at Plymouth. Well, my orders bid me sail from Plymouth on the 13th so down the coast I come, with Masters, my bos'n, for first lieutenant, and God damn me if you're not off on a cruise to Lord knows where.'

'But – you'll pardon me, sir – I fail to understand why you should –'

'I'll tell you,' Barrington cut in. 'But two things first. You're acting lieutenant in *Curlew*. I've the vice-admiral's permission for that. And for the second thing, *Curlew*'s a pretty darling and she'll outsail any vessel in the Fleet but we ain't one of your spit-and-polish frigates. When you and I are off duty as we are now, we'll drop the sirs and misters, if you please. And to make that clear we'll drink to old acquaintance.'

He crouched his way to a locker on the bulkhead and produced bottle and glasses. The wine was a Bual Madeira, and when they had clinked glasses Barrington set his elbows on the cabin table and stared thoughtfully at his new acting lieutenant.

'My orders are marked "most secret" ', he said, 'but I don't see how they can be carried out without your knowing 'em. I'm to take on board a spy and land him on the French coast by night.'

'A spy?'

'That's what I'd call him. "Emissary of His Majesty's Government" is his handle in the orders, and they've given him a by-name, Taurus. He's to arrive in Plymouth sometime today, how or whence I don't know.'

'Where are you to land him?' asked Mr Fitton, sipping his wine.

'Place called Perenno, a league and a half west of Roscoff. Never heard of it myself. And that –' Barrington wagged a finger at his companion – 'is why I've been chasin' you, Fitton. You were in *Eolus* when she was chartin' that coast. You put into Perenno two years ago with the boats from *Fortitude*. What's more, you speak the lingo and that might come in useful. I put it to Captain Frisby at Portsmouth that you were essential to success and got him to agree. So there you have it.'

He sat back with the air of a man who has rid himself of a heavy responsibility. As well he might, Mr Fitton told himself. It was typical of Admiralty to expect a young lieutenant with no knowledge of the Brittany coast to locate an inconspicuous cove like that of Perenno by night. He himself wouldn't find it easy.

'You have a set time for this landing?' he asked.

'Between midnight and four bells of the morning watch on the fourteenth.'

'That's two days past full moon.'

Barrington nodded. 'You'll need some light to bring us into Perenno, as I hope you'll do.'

'I was thinking of the battery on Pointe St Michel, commanding the bay,' Mr Fitton said.

'It commands the bay no more. A landing-party from *Pallas* shoved the 32-pounder over the cliff and it ain't been replaced – or so Frisby says.'

'And we sail tomorrow forenoon?'

'Assumin' this Taurus feller shows up, I shall cast off at first light. With a name like that on board,' Barrington added, 'it's a shame we ain't comin' out down Spithead.'

'Why so?'

'Why, because then we could watch how he behaves when we're passin' Cowes.'

Barrington's laugh was like a horse's neigh. Mr Fitton, grinning, remembered an occasion aboard *Vestal* when he had beaten Bony for making bad puns.

'What are our orders after landing Taurus?' he asked.

'Nor'-west round the Lizard – without delay, of course – for a damned silly cruise in St George's Channel – patrolling between St Ann's Head and Cork

Harbour.' Barrington rolled his eyes heavenwards. 'God save their precious Lordships and give 'em wits! I suppose they think the Frogs'll try another Irish expedition like the one that got blown off the coast in December. If they did, what's a 12-gun cutter going to do about it?' He hoisted himself to his feet, stooping under the deckhead. 'Come on, Fitton – I'd better make you acquainted with *Curlew* before Taurus shows his horns.'

Their tour of the cutter did not take long. Fo'c'sle mess-deck, galley, store-room, powder-room – all were much reduced miniatures of a frigate's accommodation. Half *Curlew*'s crew of forty-eight men were ashore on short leave, but the remaining half were yarning happily in the tiny mess-deck; according to Barrington they were a willing crowd and knew their duty. Mr Fitton was introduced to Masters the boatswain, a gypsy-looking man who seemed young for his rating; to Mr Tibbs the bald-headed carpenter; to Fidel the cook, dark-skinned and sleek, who grinned delightedly when his captain described him as the best hand with figgy duff that ever stirred a basin.

'If our passenger comes aboard in time,' Barrington said as they went up to the rainswept deck, 'we'll dine *à trois* in my cabin and you shall sample the duff. This'll be a new rig to you,' he added, jerking a thumb at the slender mast and its cordage.

Mr Fitton had plenty of experience of the fore-and-aft rig in smaller craft and the sheets and halyards of *Curlew*'s mainsail, three jibs, and square topsail presented no problems to him, though he was momentarily surprised to see a long and massive tiller in place of the wheel he was accustomed to. They walked quickly along the row of guns, eight 4-pounders and four 6-pounders.

'Can't man both broadsides at once, but it's long odds we'll never need 'em,' Barrington said. 'If there's any shootin' it'll be me with Joe Copley's gun.' He sniffed the wet air. 'Where's the wind?'

'East-sou'-east, sir. I'd say it will hold.'

'If it does it's fair enough for our course, Mr Fitton. By the by,' he went on as they walked to the after-hatch, 'the draft officer sent me a leading seaman from *Iris*, big Welshman. Seems a good hand.'

'That will be Evans,' Mr Fitton nodded. 'A first-rate seaman. His brother was killed when *Iris* boarded the *Garonne* corvette.'

'Ay? Heard a bit of that tale at Portsmouth. I'll have the rest of it from you later. – That's your cabin, larboard side of the alleyway. T'other's the byre for Taurus.'

Barrington's neighing laugh resounded as he ducked into his own cabin.

The wooden hutch which was Mr Fitton's new home had six square feet of deck-space, half of which was taken up by the wooden berth, and its headroom was just sufficient for him to stand erect with his chin on his chest; but he settled himself in it with the deepest satisfaction. *Curlew* was manifestly a happy ship and he was fortunate to join her. As for his acting-lieutenancy, in which rank his rating allowed him to do temporary duty, he entertained no great hopes from it. It was a post he had filled more than once before without obtaining the longed-for confirmation, and a 12-gun cutter was unlikely to provide opportunity for distinguishing himself in action. He stowed his volume of Epictetus and other small belongings in the locker on the bulkhead and hung up his sword and cloak, reflecting the while on tomorrow night's operation.

He knew that Mr Pitt and his Secretary for War maintained a number of secret agents whom they were fond of spiriting across the Channel to make contact with any dissident Royalists in revolutionary France. It was to be presumed that Taurus was one of these. Mr

Fitton, who had seen something of the Royalist rebels on an abortive landing two years ago, was inclined to doubt that they could achieve anything against the Jacobin rulers – if indeed any supporters of King Louis were still alive and active; the Government's clumsy attempts to assist a Royalist rising had all been miserable failures. It was curious that the Perenno cove, which he had entered on a cutting-out expedition, should have been selected for landing Taurus. The selection of a specific place and time, he thought, suggested that the emissary was to be met there by representatives of some rebel group. No doubt Taurus himself would enlighten them as to that.

The ever-present buzz of talk and laughter from the mess-deck for'ard was topped by louder voices on deck that sounded like challenge and response, and he heard Barrington go up the companion-ladder. A moment later Barrington's voice shouted his name, and he hurried on deck.

A man was just stepping on board from the quay. Though it had stopped raining he was heavily muffled in a long black cloak, and his hat was pulled down on his forehead.

'Our passenger, Mr Fitton,' Barrington said as he came up. 'Mr – um – Taurus, allow me to present my second-in-command.'

'I'm uncommon happy to renew our acquaintance, Mr Fitton,' said Colonel Tate.

2

By the light of the lamp in the captain's cabin, which was just now serving as a dining-room, Colonel Tate's long angular face looked yellower and more deeply furrowed than Mr Fitton remembered it. He was raising his glass to Barrington, who sat opposite him at the table.

'To you, captain,' he pronounced grandiloquently,

'with my thanks for a mighty fine dinner. Your figgy duff – it's so you name it? – beats pumpkin pie for refecting a weary traveller.'

'You've travelled far today?' inquired Barrington politely.

The colonel drank and set down his empty glass. 'From Taunton today, sir. Your posting service is tolerably fast. I was in Bristol at noon yesterday.'

'Bristol?' Barrington repeated.

'I had confidential business in the West Country. And speaking of business, captain, maybe we can now settle the plan for tomorrow night.'

'In one moment, sir.' Barrington raised his voice. 'Gully!'

A short and very broad seaman, who had evidently been waiting in the alleyway, dashed into the cabin, swept the remains of the meal deftly on to a tray, and dashed out again, closing the door behind him. Barrington poured wine into the three glasses.

'And now, colonel,' he said blithely, 'we're cleared for action. Fire away – Mr Fitton and I are all ears.'

The interval between Colonel Tate's arrival and dinner in the cabin had been a busy one for the acting lieutenant. The two dozen liberty men had all returned on board, most of them half-drunk but none of them incapable. When these had been dealt with, all hands were piped to ready the cutter for sea, Mr Fitton, supervising this familiar operation, found his orders obeyed promptly and efficiently, though the unwanted presence of their passenger tended to interfere with the work. The colonel, having made himself at home in his cabin, seemed to think he could do the same on deck. He wandered about chatting with the men, particularly with Sam Evans whom he remembered from his brief stay aboard *Iris*, until to Mr Fitton's relief Barrington came on deck and took him below. Ten minutes later Barrington was back.

'That American feller's a damned busybody,' he had said as they made a final round of *Curlew*'s stays and sheets and halyards. 'I suppose it's what you'd expect of a spy. But what's this about your rescuing him from a French corvette?'

Mr Fitton had replied with a very brief account of his first meeting with Colonel Tate, making no mention of his own probably unfounded suspicions.

'Busybody or not, he ain't shy,' had been Barrington's comment. 'It's a bold spy that'll go back where he's been spotted and taken before.'

Remembering that remark in the lamplit cabin after dinner, Mr Fitton was wondering that the colonel had made no attempt to disguise himself. With his long white hair, strongly marked features and tall thin body, he was a conspicuous figure. According to his own account, it was in Brest that the authorities had discovered the innocent American tourist to be an impostor; now he was to land again at Perenno, a dozen miles overland from Brest. He displayed no consciousness of temerity, however, as he leaned an elbow on the cabin table and stabbed a bony forefinger at *Curlew*'s captain to emphasize his remarks.

'Secrecy, sir,' he said impressively, 'the utmost secrecy, is the marrow of our business. I call myself Taurus. I shall call the gentleman in London who charged me with this mission Lord X. It's by the order of Lord X that I carry a message of the highest importance to a certain nobleman, a French anti-Jacobin, who goes under the by-name of Fleur-de-lys.' He cleared his throat portentously and swivelled his forefinger towards Mr Fitton. 'I guess our friend here has told you of my doings as a presoomed nootral in Brittany?'

'He has given me a *résumé* of your adventures – yes.'

Barrington's pronunciation of the word as *résoomé* might or might not have been intentional. Mr Fitton, restraining a grin, decided to indulge his own curiosity.

'What I didn't tell you, sir,' he said, 'was that Colonel Tate has a daring plan for a terrorist raid into France – a small army of jail-birds acting like American Indians on the war-path.' He turned to the colonel. 'If you'll allow me to ask it, sir, did you in fact place your plan before Lord X?'

For a moment Colonel Tate seemed disconcerted, and his large pale eyes flickered quickly from one to the other of the two officers. Then a slow smile spread across his furrowed cheeks.

' 'pears you took my little jest for earnest, my friend,' he drawled. 'No, no – 'twas something more than a wildcat scheme I had for Lord X. My investigations in the neighbourhood of Brest had revealed to me the secret existence of a force of Royalists, gentlemen, headed by the proscribed aristocrat who calls himself Fleur-de-lys. I was carrying a message from Fleur-de-lys to your government when I was intercepted by the corvette *Garonne* – which vessel, by the grace of a beneficent Providence, was taken by your *Iris*.'

'And now you're carryin' the reply to that message?' Barrington said as he paused. 'Dundas is goin' to give aid to another Breton insurrection?'

The colonel took a prolonged sip of his wine before replying.

'I calculate, captain,' he said in measured tones, 'to have told you as much as is necessary. To say more would be a breach, sir, of the secrecy to which I am bound. Suffice it that a place and time was appointed by Fleur-de-lys in the event I was able to bring a reply.'

Barrington nodded. 'Tomorrow night, the Perenno cove, between midnight and four bells morning watch.'

'If, as I presoome, that last means two o'clock in the morning, you are right, captain.'

'With your leave, colonel,' Mr Fitton said curiously, 'may I ask why Perenno was chosen as a landing-place?'

'You may ask, my friend,' returned the colonel,

flicking a glance at him, 'but I cannot tell you. I imagine Perenno is handy to the secret headquarters of Fleur-de-lys and that I am to be conducted thither. As you may know, the inland terrain of Brittany is mainly a wilderness of rocks and swamps and thickets. Now. As to the manner of my landing –'

'Belay there a second, colonel,' Barrington interposed. 'A landing may not be possible, y'know. A thick sea-mist, or a northerly gale, could prevent it.'

'In such case, sir, we make the approach on the following night. I have it from Fleur-de-lys that he will await me there on three successive nights. But the weather is likely to remain fair, they tell me.'

'We'll hope they're right. We need to make a recognisable landfall before nightfall. And by-the-by, colonel, Mr Fitton here will find Perenno for us. He's been there before.'

'He has?' Colonel Tate was mildly surprised. 'That's mighty fortunate. But I must ask your close attention, gentlemen, to the orders I've been given concerning my landing.'

Barrington raised an eyebrow. 'Orders? From this Fleur-de-lys feller?'

For some reason the innocent question seemed to excite the colonel's anger. He jutted his long jaw and his eyes sparkled with the light that Mr Fitton had once thought suggested madness.

'I'm accustomed to give orders, sir, not to take them! William Tate was born to command!' He appeared to recollect himself. 'But that's as may be. These orders must be obeyed, for the safety of all consarned. At this Perenno cove, as I understand, there is a small stone jetty at the foot of steep cliffs. A small path mounts from the jetty to two or three shacks, fishermen's cottages, on the cliff-top. The cottages are deserted and the jetty unused.' He turned to Mr Fitton. 'Am I correct, sir?'

'To the best of my knowledge – yes.'

'Very well. Your boat will come in to the jetty at the appointed hour and not more than three men will land from it – Fleur-de-lys insists upon that. Accompanied by two of your men, then, I am to advance halfway up the path.'

'That's a little odd, surely,' Barrington put in. 'You'd think he'd want you to advance on your own.'

Colonel Tate shrugged and spread his hands. 'Don't ask me for reasons, sir. Recollect that these Royalist rebels go in fear for their lives and take their precautions accordingly. And I guess we had better conform, or the reception party might loose off a musket at us.'

'As you say,' Barrington nodded. 'And they're to meet you halfway on this cliff path?'

'Yes, captain. I am to give the password, which is "Taurus", after which I shall be escorted to their camp. The two men from *Curlew* will return to the boat. Your part in our little operation is done.'

'And yours is begun,' said Barrington. 'By God, colonel, you're a bold feller! Allow me to fill your glass.'

The colonel smiled complacently. 'I am accustomed to the taking of risks, sir. Danger, sir, is the spur of all great minds.' He took a drink of wine and leaned forward. 'A last important point – the two men who land with me. One of them, I opine, should be Mr Fitton here. I figure 'twould be as well to have someone along who speaks fluent French as I'm told he does. I can get my tongue round the lingo after a fashion but I'm slow at the uptake.'

Barrington glanced at Mr Fitton, who nodded. 'Very well, colonel.'

'The other man,' the colonel continued, 'might be one of your seamen. I've a heavy valise with me, captain, as you may have noticed, and a hand to carry it up that path would be mighty useful. Such a man as –' he turned to the acting lieutenant, 'there was a big man on board *Iris*, now on board here.'

'Evans, sir?'

'That is the name. He'd make light of that valise.'

Barrington glanced at the little chronometer on the bulkhead and finished his wine.

'That's settled, then, colonel,' he said. 'Evans and Mr Fitton will land with you. And now, by your leave, we'd best turn in. There won't be much sleep for us tomorrow night. You've set an anchor-watch, Mr Fitton?'

'Yes, sir. To be relieved at eight bells.'

'See Mr Masters, if you please, and tell him he's to pipe all hands at eight bells mornin' watch – we'll put to sea as soon as maybe after that.'

'Aye, aye, sir.'

As Mr Fitton made his way on deck he was reflecting that the advent of Taurus had banished his previous flimsy suspicions. Colonel Tate remained a somewhat enigmatic character still, but the fact that London had entrusted him with this mission surely confirmed his bona fides. But who, he wondered, had told the colonel that he spoke fluent French?

3

Mr Fitton had sailed in frigates, 74s, brigs, and (as prize-master) in a French *chasse-marée*, but none of them had provided him with the sheer joy of sailing he found in *Curlew*. The big cutter, with her vast spread of canvas on the single mast and her quick response to the slightest movement of the tiller, deserved her captain's affectionate encomiums. It took him a little time to get used to the steep heel of the narrow deck and to realize how much closer to the wind she could sail than the square-riggers he was accustomed to, but by the time she had covered half of her 120-mile passage he was as

Secret Emissary

much at home with his vessel's ways as a good sea-officer should be.

They had put Drake's Island astern while it was yet dark, and the growing light of a grey February morning found them heading due south with a steady wind from east-south-east. On a wind the cutter was at her best point of sailing. The sea was slight, its ridged waves white-crested by the breeze, and she flew across it beneath the clouded sky more like a bird than a boat, her plumage of mains'l, square tops'l, and three jibs arching wing-like as the wind filled it. With so steady a breeze and the dark horizon clear on every hand there was little work for the watch-on-deck, and she sped on and on without a sheet being touched. A cast of the log gave her ten-and-a-half knots.

'I'd give 'em a spell of gun-drill if she had five degrees less heel,' Lieutenant Barrington told his second-in-command as they stood together at the rail. 'As it is, we'll wait till we can bring the wind astern.' His eye fell on a pair of seagulls who were cruising hopefully above *Curlew*'s wake. 'No reason why I shouldn't have a bit of practice myself, though.'

He went below and returned a few minutes later carrying his sporting-gun.

'Loaded and at half-cock,' he announced. 'See this? A cap goes under the hammer and the touch-hole's beneath it. Damned ingenious, eh?'

He eased the hammer back with his thumb and put the gun to his shoulder, moving the barrel to follow the swooping and swaying of one of the gulls. There was a loud report and the gull dropped into the sea. Its fall was followed by cheers from the watching hands up for'ard.

'Belay that!' Barrington yelled. 'Any shoutin' aboard this ship I'll do myself! – Twenty fathom range, I'd say,' he added more quietly.

'It was a good shot,' Mr Fitton said with sincerity.

Barrington, watching the remaining gull recover from its fright and resume its cruising astern, replaced the ramrod he had taken from its clips on the gun.

'No,' he decided. 'It's too easy takin' 'em bows-on. It's when they come whizzin' over, Fitton – mark cock! You've a split second to judge your aim and the target's crossin' overhead at thirty knots – that's a sportin' shot, if you like.'

Mr Fitton could admire his captain's marksmanship but he was glad the second gull had been spared; he himself would have shot for the pot but not solely for the sake of hitting a living target. It had just occurred to him that it was odd that he should have no objection to firing a gun at a Frenchman when he became aware that Colonel Tate had come on deck. The colonel had remained in his cabin until now, and the greenish hue of his deeply lined face was evidence of the slight *mal-de-mer* that had kept him there. The reason for the shot, whose sound had brought him up, was explained to him, and Barrington's enthusiasm for his Copley gun led to a long discussion of firearms, which ended in the two of them going below to examine a brace of pistols. Mr Fitton, whose watch it was, remained on deck.

'As she goes,' Barrington said as he departed. 'Call me if there's any change in the wind.'

'Aye aye, sir.'

But there was no variation in the strong steady breeze, and throughout the afternoon watch *Curlew* continued to eat up her southing without diminution of speed. Halfway through the watch the colonel reappeared on deck and after exchanging a word with Mr Fitton stalked away for'ard to chat with the seamen of the watch. He went below again after a while, and a few minutes later Leading Seaman Evans came aft and knuckled his forehead in salute.

'Well, Evans?' Mr Fitton said. 'That jib-sheet chafing again?'

'Nay, sir – she's clear an' free now.' Evans hesitated a moment. ' 'Tis a word or two the – the passenger let fall just now.'

'Colonel Tate? He seems fond of talking to you, Sam.'

They were far enough from the two steersmen at the tiller for quiet conversation to be unheard.

'Aye,' Sam said. 'Seems interested in the part o' the world I come from. Wonderin' how I come to know the Pembroke coast so well, me that was up an' down from Dinas Head to St David's when I was a whippersnapper. But from what he said a minute ago, sir, seemed he was expectin' me to go ashore with him tonight. Would that be gospel, now?'

'Yes. You'll have the order from Mr Barrington in due course.'

It was unnecessary to go into detail. In a vessel of *Curlew*'s size the whole ship's company would know of Colonel Tate's landing and its purpose by now.

'You and I are to land with Mr Tate,' Mr Fitton continued, 'and go up the path with him until he meets a reception party. You'll be required to help with his valise. It's not a leading seaman's job but you won't turn it down, I hope.'

Sam answered Mr Fitton's grin with another.

'Not me, sir. Happy to set foot ashore in Frog country.'

'Very well.'

Sam touched his forehead and rejoined the rest of his watch, who were squatting under the weather-rail for'ard.

The cutter raced on towards the French coast, now less than thirty miles ahead. Barrington, coming on deck to relieve his acting lieutenant at the end of the afternoon watch, sent a lookout to the masthead and after consulting with Mr Fitton altered course half-a-point eastward. Traverse board and chart between them suggested that unless *Curlew* had made more leeway than estimated she would make her first landfall of the Isle of Batz; off Roscoff.

It was five minutes after Mr Fitton had come on deck again to take the last dog-watch when the masthead hailed to report land ahead.

'Down you come, Spragg!' Mr Fitton shouted; there was not room for more than one man at the cutter's masthead.

He tucked the telescope which Barrington had supplied into his pocket and jumped into the weather shrouds as Spragg landed on the deck. The narrowing ladder of the shrouds had no ample platform at its top, but the cap of the mainmast gave him footing and the topmast was slim enough to hook an arm round. The big straining quadrilateral of the topsail would have interrupted his view if *Curlew* had had the wind astern, but close-hauled as she now was he could see past the weather leech of the sail. Under the clouded sky of early evening the horizon was dark and clear ahead, and the land was no more than a thickening of that dark line. It was some minutes, and the French coast had risen noticeably higher, before he could decide positively that a just discernible projection of the coast was in fact the island he expected to see.

He clambered down the shrouds, Spragg starting aloft again as he touched deck, and reported to the waiting Barrington.

'A good landfall, sir. Isle of Batz one point on the larboard bow.'

'The chart, then, in my cabin.' Barrington raised his voice. 'Mr Masters! In tops'l and flying jib and take a reef in the mains'l. – We'll come no closer in to Roscoff than we have to,' he added as they went below.

Colonel Tate, who was suffering from a return of his seasickness, was still in his cabin. Barrington put in his head to inform him of the landfall and was answered by an inarticulate grunt. The chart was spread on the cabin table, and the dead-reckoning position Barrington had marked on it proved to correspond nicely with Mr Fitton's bearing of the Isle de Batz. Perenno was now nine miles away to the south-west, and they laid a course west by south. *Curlew*, with sail reduced and the wind over her larboard quarter, held on more slowly keeping the land just in sight. Spragg at the masthead had been warned to keep his eyes open extra wide, for French coasting craft or even a privateer might be met with. But there seemed to be no sea-borne activity along this short stretch of coast, and when the cutter altered course to close the shore they had not sighted so much as a fishing-boat.

Evening had come early, darkening land and sea to planes of dead black and shifting grey, but Mr Fitton had no difficulty in recognizing the shape of the low hill that rose inland and west of the Perenno cove. It was unnecessary to come any nearer. *Curlew* turned away northward until the Brittany coast was a low blur on the rim of a shadowy sea and then hove-to to wait for midnight.

4

The middle watch, between midnight and four in the morning, had always seemed to Mr Fitton to hold a double hazard. There was the ineluctable curtain of the blackest hours of night, defeating sight and rendering the movement of friend or enemy invisible. But behind this his imagination pictured a hidden struggle, as if some angel of darkness strove furiously to hold back the progress that would propel the world into dawn and sunrise. The sense of an inimical presence behind the screen of night was with him now, as *Curlew*'s boat pulled into the rocky jaws of the Perenno cove. It was a natural enough feeling, he told himself, when they were closing an enemy shore.

He sat with an arm over the tiller, sharing the stern thwart with Colonel Tate, who was unwontedly silent. The colonel had recovered sufficiently from his *mal-de-mer* to eat and drink before leaving the cutter, and appeared ready to face his shore adventure with equanimity. Since this was the smaller of *Curlew*'s two boats only four men were needed to man her; Evans and Drew pulled stroke oars, Sims and Bronski pulled in the bows. Cutlasses had been served out to the cutter's men including Mr Fitton, and they lay on the bottom-boards with the colonel's valise. Barrington had brought *Curlew* to within half-a-mile of the shore, but when Mr Fitton looked astern for a sight of her she was already invisible in the obscurity.

It was two years since he had put into the narrow Perenno bay on that abortive cutting-out expedition, but its dimly-seen features were well remembered. The black bulk of Pointe St Michel to larboard, the rocky islet of Le Cornic a ghostly silhouette to starboard. A thick ceiling of cloud hid the moon, which in any case was too low to top the cliffs rising at the head of the cove, and it was impossible to make out any details on the wall of broken rock towards which they were pulling. It was like a sheer wall of jet standing above a rippled pool of ink. Hard to believe that a path climbed it, and that halfway up that path – if all was as it should be – a party of men awaited them. By now those men must have seen the boat on the faintly luminous surface below them. He recalled that it was at least a fortnight since Colonel Tate had received instructions from Fleur-de-lys; the Royalists might have been rounded-up or wiped out in the interim.

'Your friends up there could have shown a light safely,' he remarked, speaking his thought aloud.

'They dare not take the slightest risk, sir,' returned the colonel. 'I believe I make out the jetty,' he added quickly. 'Remember, my friend – only three of us must land.'

'I'll remember,' Mr Fitton said somewhat impatiently. 'Shorten stroke, men.'

He had already seen the jetty, a little square of paler darkness at eye-level half-a-cable away, and was steering for it. It was half-tide, the cove was completely sheltered from the wind, and the small waves lapping the stone of the jetty wall were no impediment to a neat sheering alongside. Evans's feet crunched on the worn steps as he landed to hold her steady while Colonel Tate climbed ashore. Mr Fitton stuck his cutlass in his belt, handed up the valise, and followed.

'Drew, you're in charge of the boat,' he said. 'Five minutes should see us back here. Colonel, you'd best lead the way.'

The stonework of the little jetty projected from the foot of a slope of broken rock. Now that they were close to the cliff it could be seen that it was of no great height and leaned back at an angle which, though steep, was not impossibly so. A path, dimly discerned, slanted up rightward from the inner end of the jetty. Mr Fitton, tilting his head far back to stare up at the featureless blackness above, could see no movement up there; the only sound that came to his ears was the ceaseless wash of waves on the stony shore that stretched on either hand.

Colonel Tate in the lead, Evans following with the valise, and Mr Fitton last in the short file, they started up the path. It was steep and rough, and the large rocks that had fallen on it in places suggested that it was not often used. They reached a roughly levelled platform where the path turned sharply up to the left, and thirty paces higher a second platform from which it mounted to the right. They had taken half-a-dozen steps up this third zigzag when a voice spoke sharply from above.

'*Halte-là!*'

They halted. The clustered shapes of men could just be made out on the corner of the path overhead.

'Taurus!' said Colonel Tate loudly.

'*Avancez*,' said the voice.

Afterwards, Mr Fitton retained only a hazy recollection of what happened next. There was a shouted oath from Evans, a rush and clatter of feet. He was lugging out his cutlass when a savage blow on his head drove all consciousness from him.

The return to life came slowly and painfully. He was half-sitting, half-reclining on a hard unstable surface, with his shoulders against something that felt like a man's knees. He groped behind him and grasped a leg.

'Who's that?' he demanded feebly.

'Drew, sir. Take it easy, sir – we're a'most back to the cutter.'

'I'm in the boat?'

'Aye, sir. Nasty crack on the head, you got.'

Mr Fitton put a hand to his head. The side of his face was wet and sticky with blood. Some inkling of recent events returned to him.

'Is Evans here?' he asked.

'No, sir,' Drew said angrily. 'Them bloody Frogs has got him.' He hesitated. 'Sir, captain's orders was not to land, but me and Bronski's been ashore. We heard Sam Evans give a shout and there was noises like a scuffle and then nothing more though we was listening for a good five minutes. I took it on meself to disobey orders and go up the path, sir.'

'Mr Barrington won't hold it against you. So you found me and carried me down?'

'We found nothing going up the path, sir. It was clear nearly to the top – I reckoned not to go right up, 'case of ambush. 'Twas coming down we spotted you, down off the path. They'd knocked you over the edge, and you was lucky your coat had caught on a rock else you'd have fallen a long way.' Drew broke off to reply to a shout from not far ahead. '*Curlew*! Mr Fitton here, wounded.'

Mr Fitton's head felt as if it was being split open but

he got himself inboard over *Curlew*'s rail unaided. Barrington gripped his arm.

'What happened, for God's sake?' he demanded.

'It was a trap. Evans and the colonel are taken.'

'God damn the – hold up, man! – Mr Tibbs! Bandages and a bowl of water to my cabin, and look lively!'

Lying in the darkness of his cabin ten minutes later, with his bandaged head throbbing in stabs of pain, Mr Fitton was in no condition for connected thought. That a force of Jacobins had been waiting for Colonel Tate in place of the expected Royalists was plain enough to his scattered wits. But how this substitution had come about, and why Sam Evans had (apparently) been taken prisoner while he himself had been left for dead, were questions he was presently incapable of formulating.

4　The Sporting Shot

1

It was four bells of the middle watch, in the small hours of St Valentine's Day, when *Curlew* shook her sails and glided away like a tall white ghost from the dark Brittany cliffs. Lieutenant Barrington was not going to linger any longer than was necessary on an enemy coast; if the Jacobins had known that a British agent was to be landed they would also know that a British vessel was somewhere in the offing. By the afternoon of that day, the wind holding fair, she had passed the Scillies and was heading northward for St Ann's Head to begin her patrol across St George's Channel.

Mr Tibbs the carpenter, whose second duty it was to act as surgeon when required, had dealt efficiently with the contused wound on the side of Mr Fitton's head and the acting lieutenant's hardy constitution had speeded his recovery. He was standing his deck-watch as usual before the cutter had sighted the English coast, with his hat settled securely over the carpenter's ample bandages. He had given Barrington his account of the ambush and the capture of Tate and Sam Evans, and they had discussed the advisability of heading back to Plymouth to report the matter. Barrington had decided against it.

'My orders,' he had declared, 'were to land this damned grass-combing agent and then proceed without delay – without delay, mark you – to my patrolling station. I've landed Tate, and lost a good seaman in doin' it, and my next duty's to carry out my orders.'

Mr Fitton had not disputed this decision; if Fleur-de-lys and his rebels had been discovered and wiped out, as seemed likely, there was no urgent need to report the capture of the British Government's agent. And, as Barrington pointed out, the incident could be reported to a senior naval officer the first time they put into Cork harbour, for *Polyphemus*, 74, was stationed at Cork. There were no Royal Navy ships in Milford Haven, which was a convenient refuge in case of storm or for taking in water.

The fate of Sam Evans worried Mr Fitton a good deal. The confusion of that sudden night assault made it impossible to say with certainty what had happened to him. The assumption that he was a prisoner of the French, with Colonel Tate, was the obvious one; but it was conceivable that he had been knocked on the head and slung over the cliff, like Mr Fitton himself. In that case Drew might have missed seeing him when he made his foray up the cliff path, and he could be lying among the rocks, perhaps alive and badly injured. It wasn't a pleasant thought. Mr Fitton had formed a liking for the big leading seaman, and he found himself – unusually – nursing a smouldering anger against spies and spy-masters in general and Colonel William Tate in particular. And when he considered Tate he found all his old suspicion of the man returning.

In the last light of that day *Curlew* made her landfall of Linney Head on the Pembrokeshire coast and felt her way into West Angle Bay to drop anchor for the night, with St Ann's Head three miles away across the mouth of the Haven. If he was supposed to be looking out for another French armada, Barrington said, there was no point in patrolling at night; they might as well make themselves comfortable. And comfortable they were in

Curlew's main cabin that evening. Fidel the cook produced a well-seasoned stew of beef and vegetables for the two officers, and after Gully had cleared the table they sat very snugly over their wine, in a lamplit cabin that swayed only gently on the waters of the sheltered bay. The wine was a sound claret, and Mr Fitton, whose head wound was less painful than it had been all day, would have been content but for his remembrance of the missing Evans. As it was, he sipped his wine and listened with half an ear to Barrington's tales of shooting-parties ashore while his thoughts ran upon the landing at Perenno.

' – and when I picked the bird up,' Barrington was saying, ending a story, 'what was it but old Lady Bourne's African parrot!' He paused and eyed his companion. 'I'd thought to win a laugh from you, Fitton, but it seems I'm talkin' to a deaf man.'

'My dear Barrington, pray accept my apologies,' Mr Fitton said sincerely. 'It's true my thoughts were elsewhere for a moment.'

'Let's have 'em, then.' Barrington poured wine into the two glasses. 'It's your turn to spin a yarn, anyway.'

Mr Fitton took a drink, hesitated a further moment, and took his decision.

'Very well,' he said, 'I'll spin you a yarn that may be a true one for all I know. It concerns an American adventurer, a soldier of fortune by his own account –'

'William Tate by name?' Barrington put in.

'I'll call him Tate, since you suggest it. This Tate, then, arrives in France and offers his services to the French. They employ him as a spy and propose to land him by night on the English coast. There he'll assume –'

'Hold on, hold on! What's he supposed to spy on?'

'Let's say he's to bring back information about our coastal defences. He'll assume the character of an American friendly to our cause, and he carries letters of introduction from notables in the United States who are also opposed to the Revolution in France. Well, the French vessel that was to land him is captured by a British frigate and Tate has to find himself a tale to explain his presence on board. He was captured, he says, when he was on his way to England with important information for the British Government. The frigate's captain accepts that story.'

Barrington was frowning very hard at his second-in-command. 'So did whoever he saw in London,' he said. 'And what's more he *did* bring important information – about this feller Fleur-de-lys.'

'I'll remind you that I'm spinning this yarn,' Mr Fitton said with half a grin. 'Tate's letters of introduction were cleverly forged. I've heard of such things being done. As for Fleur-de-lys, there may be a rebel leader of that name or Tate may simply have invented him. Did Tate tell you who he saw in London?'

'Some underling of Dundas, who's Secretary of State for War.' Barrington pointed a sudden finger. 'You're not puttin' this forward as fact?'

'I'm spinning a yarn, as requested. Here's the rest of it. Tate has a fortnight in which to do whatever he has to do in England. It includes what he calls "some confidential business in the West Country", and takes him to Bristol. His claim that he has to bear the Government's reply back to Fleur-de-lys wins him a naval vessel to transport him to Perenno and the bosom of his French Jacobin friends.' Mr Fitton sat back and picked up his glass. 'Well, that's my tale. You'll say it's an unlikely one. But is it any more unlikely than Tate's own story, Barrington?'

'Gad's me life!' Barrington was staring goggle-eyed. 'D'you believe this yarn of yours?'

'Why not? And there are other things.' He told of the discrepancies he and Evans had noticed after the taking of the *Garonne*. 'My story explains all those.'

'It don't explain how Tate could arrange for an

ambush to be waitin' for us at Perenno, Fitton. And how about all that hocus-pocus of passwords and only three men to land and so forth?'

'Just hocus-pocus, as you say,' returned Mr Fitton, though without much conviction. 'By the by,' he added, 'it was you, I suppose, who told the colonel I could speak French?'

'I? No – never had a chance to mention it. Why?'

'Just that it's another odd thing about Colonel Tate, that's all.'

Mr Fitton relapsed into frowning silence. Barrington, his bony face screwed into a scowl, appeared to be considering what he had heard. In the pause a burst of laughter sounded from the mess-deck for'ard. It seemed to rouse Barrington from his meditations.

'Far as I can see, Fitton,' he said slowly, 'the matter's finished with. Even if your yarn's a true one there's nothing we can do about it now. My only concern is that Colonel damn-his-eyes Tate has made off with one of my crew – that's if he's what you make him out to be.' He tossed the last of his wine down his throat. 'To hell with Colonel Tate, say I! Let's talk of something else. Tell you what, Fitton – I'm determined to get some shootin' this cruise. When we come in to Cork –'

Lieutenant Barrington, it transpired, had no intention of wasting the sporting opportunities offered by what he regarded as a useless patrol duty. He had not before entered Cork harbour, but he had learned from charts and pilot manuals that it was entered by a long and narrow estuary. There would be waterfowl, duck or geese perhaps, that could be taken in flight. Pity there wasn't a second gun for Fitton. And Milford Haven might show sport as well. Refilling *Curlew*'s water-casks was a perfectly good excuse for putting into Milford. Daybreak was the time for wild-fowling, and if they used the cockboat –

Mr Fitton, listening with concealed amusement to this

and much more of the same kind, reflected that it might not amuse their Lordships at the Admiralty if they learned that one of their warships was being used as a seaborne shooting-lodge. To the philosophic mind, however, it must surely be less reprehensible to shoot wildfowl than to slaughter Frenchmen. His wounded head was beginning to throb by the time Barrington had finished an enthusiastic lecture on the lock of his Copley gun; and he was glad when his senior suggested that it was time for them both to turn in.

The wind backed to the south-west in the night, and it was blowing hard when *Curlew* sailed out from the shelter of her anchorage on the first of her patrols. She had sailed at two bells of the morning watch, and by noon, in moderating weather, was halfway on her crossing of 120 sea-miles and shaking out the reef in her mainsail. It was no weather for a masthead lookout in a cutter, but Barrington had posted a man in the bows as a somewhat perfunctory concession to his orders. In fact, they saw no sail after leaving the Pembroke coast until they came within the ambit of Cork's busy coastal traffic.

Mr Fitton found himself in charge of the deck for most of the day's sailing, Barrington being much occupied in instructing and overseeing Mr Tibbs. The carpenter was constructing a wooden rack against the after rail, a kind of ready-use locker (as Barrington explained) for the Copley shotgun. Here the gun, loaded, could be placed under a canvas spray-cover ready to be seized and fired should any sporting target present itself. It was completed before sunset, at which time *Curlew* was close in to the low green shores on either side of the narrow entrance to Cork harbour. But her captain was to have no opportunity of using his gun in the estuary beyond. *Polyphemus* lay at anchor just inside the entrance, and the cutter had not been in sight of her for five minutes when the signal flags at the 74's

The Sporting Shot

yardarm summoned her captain to come on board. *Curlew*'s boat took Barrington across while Mr Fitton saw to her anchoring; a lieutenant didn't keep a post-captain waiting and Captain Matthews was said to be a martinet in such matters.

Twilight had fallen before Barrington returned. He beckoned the acting lieutenant down to his cabin.

'Trust a post-captain to find work for a fast cutter when he gets his claws on one,' he said. 'Matthews hardly listened to my report of Tate's capture. I'm to carry his dispatches back to Milford. There's an Admiralty agent there and he'll send them on, post, to London. They won't be sent on board till tomorrow, though.'

'Giving time for some shooting?' suggested Mr Fitton.

Barrington wagged his head ruefully. 'Not while I'm waitin' for dispatches that could be urgent. There's been a scare over here, Fitton. These God-damned Irish have been discovered musterin' and drillin' in secret – brigs laden with military stores hidden in creeks. Had it from Black, third lieutenant. *Polyphemus*'s men were out two days ago with the garrison infantry, roundin' up the last of 'em. They had French officers, Black says, and it's thought they planned to land on the Welsh coast. But I'll get my shootin', never fear. Once we're back in Milford Haven we'll have the boat overside, and if there's any duck to be had we'll have 'em. And that'll be tomorrow mornin', Fitton.'

But this rash prophecy was not to be fulfilled.

It was after noon when *Polyphemus*'s boat brought the dispatches across to *Curlew*, and in the interval the wind had backed easterly and fallen away to a fitful breeze, a head-wind for the cutter's course back to the Haven. It was daybreak before she rounded St Ann's Head and two hours more before she had berthed alongside the quay at Milford. Then Mr Cadwallader, the Admiralty's agent, was discovered to have deserted Milford for more comfortable lodgings in Haverfordwest and Barrington had to hire a chaise to take him there. Messengers riding post would take the dispatches by way of Carmarthen and Bristol to London – a long road but much shorter than the route by sea.

Mr Fitton made opportunity to inquire along the quays for Will Devonald and his brig, but the smuggler was not in port. *Olwen*, he was told, was expected back from 'somewheres to south'rd' in two or three days. He was not surprised to find that the news of the intended raid from Ireland and its suppression had already reached Milford; there were many trading vessels passing between Cork and the Haven.

It was late in the afternoon when Barrington got back from Haverfordwest.

'Mr damn-his-eyes Cadwallader needs a charge of gunpowder in his breeches,' he told Mr Fitton, 'but the dispatches are on their way. So are we – over to our anchorage in West Angle Bay. For by hell's fires, Fitton, I'm goin' to get my shootin' before we sail tomorrow!'

So it came about that in the first grey light of a mild February morning *Curlew*'s boat was pulling gently over a glimmer of little waves a quarter-mile off the northern shores of the bay. In the bows Barrington nursed his loaded shotgun, in the sternsheets Mr Fitton sat with the musket Barrington had insisted on his bringing – 'if a greylag comes over you might bag it' – and on the midships thwart the boatswain plied a pair of sculls. Masters had applied for this task on the ground that he was country bred and liked a bit o' sport. There was hardly any wind to dispel the mists that writhed, slowly lifting, from the sea's surface, now and then revealing a glimpse of the shore. They had been on the alert for half-an-hour without seeing a single bird, not so much as a seagull.

The three mallard that flashed suddenly out of the mist came from the offshore side, so there was some excuse for Barrington's slowness. He flung up his gun, but before he could settle the butt against his shoulder the ducks had vanished into the shoreward mists. The first syllable of an oath was cut short by a yell from Masters.

'Mark cock!'

A smaller bird flying straight and high had appeared heading shoreward. Barrington's muzzle followed it in a swift arc and he pulled trigger. The bird seemed to explode in a flurry of blue-grey feathers and dropped into the sea a biscuit-toss from the boat.

'By God that was shootin', though I say it myself!' Barrington exulted. 'That's what I call a sportin' shot, Fitton.'

Masters, with a couple of strokes, had brought the boat within reach of the floating bird and Mr Fitton took it from the water.

'It's a pigeon,' he said. 'And there's a ring on its leg – a carrier pigeon, I suppose.'

'No, sir, by your leave,' Masters said. 'Carrier's a different sort. That's a homing pigeon. Carry messages a hundred mile and more, they will. Here, sir – use this.'

He pulled a knife from its leather sheath on his belt and passed it to Mr Fitton, who was trying to undo the thin twine that bound a strip of oiled silk to the pigeon's leg. The silk, unrolled, revealed a tiny slip of paper. The writing on it was minute but clear: '*Légion Noire NVP*'.

2

Mr Fitton was afterwards to ask himself whether his Tutelary Genius (who had, conceivably, contrived this chance-in-a-thousand) had thought to present him, in the shape of that slip of paper, with the key to the whole mystery of Colonel Tate. If so, the Genius must have been disappointed in his disciple. The message instantly brought to mind the colonel's fantastic talk, on board *Iris*, of a terrorist raid – 'call 'em the Black Legion' – but a more sinister implication came from the remark made by the successful marksman.

'That little feller won't give us a pigeon pie,' said Barrington, laying down his gun and stepping aft. 'Drop him overboard, bos'n. What's the message he was carryin'?'

Pigeon pie. The phrase woke a thought so incredible that Mr Fitton automatically rejected it.

'It's in French,' he replied, handing over the paper. 'Black Legion NVP. I don't know what it means.'

'It means it was being sent to a Frenchman, Fitton,' Barrington said, frowning. 'It's long odds one of their damned spies sent it. Nothing we can do about it, far as I can see.'

'It had better be reported,' Mr Fitton said slowly.

'I'll log it, anyway.' Barrington dropped the slip into his pocket. 'What's the time?'

Mr Fitton consulted his watch. 'Coming up to six bells, sir.'

'Gad's me life! We'd best get back to duty. Mr Masters, I'll thank you to pull back to the ship.'

Half an hour later *Curlew* slipped out of West Angle Bay and headed westward again for Cork.

That day's uneventful crossing, enlivened only by an hour of gun-drill, marked the beginning of an almost unprecedented spell of fine weather. Blue skies and a blue sea told of a spring come before its time, and though the wind stayed in the east there was warmth enough in the sun to soften its bite. At Cork, Barrington, who went on board *Polyphemus* to report the delivery of Captain Matthews's dispatches, received an invitation to dine in the 74's wardroom and so had to abandon his plan for an evening's shooting in the Cork estuary. Next day on the eastward run Mr Tibbs, having examined Mr Fitton's head wound, decreed that the bandaging could now be replaced by a plaster. A light and contrary wind delayed the cutter's arrival in the Haven and the Copley gun developed a fault in its lock. Barrington announced that *Curlew* would refill her water-casks next time she put in to Milford, and that there would then be shore leave for all hands. Throughout these minor happenings, the routine of shipboard, and his duties as deck-officer, Mr Fitton was struggling against a conviction that forced itself ever more strongly upon him. He knew it was irrational to fight against it; and in the end – it was when *Curlew* was halfway on her third westward crossing of St George's Channel – he resolved to apply reason to his doubts and apprehensions.

It was towards the end of the afternoon watch, his watch-on-deck, and Barrington was below decks. The boatswain was for'ard with a party overhauling the anchor-cable, and Mr Fitton drew him aside.

'In the matter of homing pigeons, Mr Masters,' he said. 'You seem knowledgeable about them.'

'Learned of 'em from my old uncle, up Liverpool way, sir,' said Masters. 'Used to run a proper fleet of 'em, he did, some as far as a pal of his in Kent. He'd tell you as how they was used as messengers as long ago as King Solomon.'

'They steer a straight course to their objective, I suppose?'

'Right you are, sir – though God knows how they do it. Spirals up, then on course, straight as an arrow.'

Barrington came on deck at that moment. Mr Fitton thanked the boatswain, and having formally handed over the deck to his captain went below. On the shelf in the main cabin was a copy of John Cary's *Atlas*. He took it down, laid it on the table, and found the map he wanted and a ruler to lay across it. When he had done this he stood motionless, staring down at the map, for a full minute. The line he had indicated with the ruler passed through Brest and the estimated spot where the pigeon had been shot; and its northward extension passed through Haverfordwest, seven miles north of which was Long Warren.

Mr Fitton went into his own cabin and sat on his bunk to think. Of course, someone in Haverfordwest might have sent that pigeon on its way to Brest. But then, what of Madame de Callac's pigeon pies, and the pigeons that had to be brought from Callac, which was only a little way north of Brest? The pigeons at Long Warren, he remembered, had been caged-in with netting. Would that have been necessary if they were not homing pigeons? And surely it was strange that an exiled French aristocrat should choose to live in a remote part of Pembrokeshire. If she was a Jacobin spy –

He broke off his thoughts with an inarticulate growl. It was difficult to think of Simone de Callac as other than she had seemed when they had sat together by the fire in the Long Warren parlour. He recalled her grace of movement, the direct gaze of her blue-grey eyes, her manner – even in their informal talk she had had the air of a lady of birth. Brief as had been their meeting, he had conceived a liking for her, and could almost feel that she, too, had – but all this had passed through his mind a dozen times and it made no difference to the web of suspicions whose threads, tenuous as they were, stretched to link so many circumstances within his knowledge. He began again on the weaving of that web.

If the Comtesse de Callac was a Jacobin spy good reason could be found for her establishment at Long Warren. The French had planned a massive invasion from Ireland in December – the Pembrokeshire coast was a likely landing-place – and Long Warren was four or five miles from the beaches of St Bride's Bay; an agent with means of sending information would be useful. The invasion attempt had been defeated by the weather, but (as they had learned from *Polyphemus*) there had been a projected raid by rebel Irish, officered by Frenchmen, detected and frustrated less than a week ago. What more likely than that an invading force from France had been intended to assist the Irish? Or that the French agent, learning of the Irish failure, would send a message to the Jacobin headquarters at Brest? News of it had reached Milford by 17 February, as he had discovered; it could have reached Long Warren too. And the pigeon carrying the message had been shot on the 18th.

Shouts from on deck told that Barrington was having the topsail hoisted, but Mr Fitton, doggedly spinning his web, scarcely heard them. The message: *Légion Noire NVP*. If it was intended to convey that the raid from Ireland had failed it was very oddly worded; but, if his other assumptions were correct, it must surely link Simone de Callac with Colonel William Tate. This might seem a long shot, he reflected, since there could be other Black Legions besides the colonel's proposed army of terrorists, but there was another circumstance to justify it. For by his own account Tate had been in Bristol 'on confidential business'; driving post across country he could have reached Long Warren — that would be a day or two after Mr Fitton's own visit — and from Long Warren a pigeon message could be sent arranging for the ambush at Perenno. Moreover, it would be from Madame de Callac that Tate had learned that Mr Fitton could speak French. Perhaps it had been his original intention to make for Pembrokeshire if the French corvette had succeeded in landing him. At any rate, on this showing there could be no doubt that Colonel Tate was an agent of the French Jacobins.

Mr Fitton shifted uneasily on the uncomfortable wooden rim of his bunk. Well, there it was, all the anomalies and mysteries explained and linked. And the linking threads were so slender that his web of explanation was as light and insubstantial as a spider's.

Put it before Barrington, see what he thought of it? It was repugnance to the idea of accusing Simone de Callac on such slender evidence that decided Mr Fitton to keep his conclusions to himself.

As he got up to go on deck he remembered that there was still a mystery for which he had found no explanation: the wording of the pigeon message. But this was instantly driven from his mind by a loud report, followed by a howl of execration, from the deck. It was only Barrington, however, who had fired at a high-flying gull and missed.

'Didn't allow for *Curlew*'s speed,' he explained as Mr Fitton came up. 'We're makin' seven knots, d'ye see, and the target was flyin' at maybe twenty knots, same direction. I'll know better next time,' he added, reloading.

But the next gulls they saw were the white flocks surrounding the boats of a fishing-fleet a mile or two off the Cork harbour entrance, and even Barrington baulked at firing so close to the men in the boats. The cutter glided in past the green headlands and dropped anchor, as she had done twice before, two cable-lengths from *Polyphemus*.

Captain Matthews had ordered *Curlew*'s captain to report on board the 74 each time he crossed from Milford, so Barrington duly had himself pulled across. He returned looking disgruntled.

'We're to make a night passage, Mr Fitton,' he said abruptly. 'See all's ready for makin' sail before sunset. Then report to my cabin, if you please.'

'Aye aye, sir.'

Ten minutes later Mr Fitton was listening to Barrington's grumbles. He had found Captain Matthews in no very good temper, owing to the non-arrival of two frigates which were supposed to be joining him from Portsmouth. The captain had peremptorily ordered him to take on board a major of

The Sporting Shot

infantry, who was very ill with some mysterious fever, and convey him to Waterford, sixty miles up the Irish coast, where the army maintained a hospital ship in the harbour.

'Turnin' *Curlew* into a bloody floatin' sick-bay!' Barrington said explosively. 'I reminded him that my orders were to patrol St George's Channel from the Haven to Cork, and he came near blowin' my head off. "It's as much St George's Channel sixty miles north as it is here, Mr Barrington!" he says. "And you'll cross it, at my order, from Waterford to St David's Head this time".'

'Haven't the military a surgeon at Cork?' Mr Fitton enquired.

'Yes, but it seems there's a feller at Waterford who's a top-sawyer with this sort of fever. He's aboard this hospital ship – a hulk, I gathered – lyin' a couple of miles up the Waterford estuary.' Barrington brightened somewhat. 'If the wind holds fair we should be comin' in at first light. Might get some shootin'.'

'And this invalid comes on board tonight?'

'Any time now. There'll be an orderly with him and they'll have to have my cabin. I'll be usin' yours for my watch-below, by your leave.'

In the event, it was half an hour after sunset when the fever-stricken major, swathed in blankets on a stretcher, was hoisted on board from one of *Polyphemus*'s boats. He was barely conscious and his attendant orderly settled him comfortably enough in Barrington's cabin. In the last light of a fine evening *Curlew* tacked out of Cork harbour and headed east-nor'-east with a fair wind and the Irish coast three miles away under her lee. By daybreak she was closing the mouth of the Waterford estuary, with Hook Head, to starboard, almost hidden in low-lying mist.

Waterford town, where one of the largest garrisons in Ireland was established, was ten miles inland and its main harbour was in fact the Suir estuary where the army's hospital ship was moored. The transhipment of the invalid occupied an hour or more, and it was eight bells of the morning watch before the cutter rounded the low green point of Hook Head and brought the Irish coast astern. With a steady breeze from sou'-sou'-east she could just hold a course east by south; a course which (as Barrington remarked) conformed exactly to Captain Matthews's order, since it would bring her to the Welsh coast a little north of St David's Head sixty miles away.

That morning – it was 22 February – the mild bright weather was more like summer than early spring. Mr Fitton, gazing astern from the after rail, saw the white line of *Curlew*'s wake stretching across the sea's furrowed blue to the fast-fading coast and admired the beauty of the scene. In retrospect he was to think of that line as the last of the many threads that had drawn him so inexorably into conflict with the Black Legion.

3

'It's very well for a feller that likes sailin',' Barrington said, 'very well indeed. But for men who're supposed to be fightin' the French it's no fun. We're about as far away from the war as we can get, Fitton.'

He scowled at the placid blue sea across which the cutter, under her full sail, was smoothly gliding.

'We came a little nearer at Cork,' Mr Fitton pointed out. 'If the Irish had got their expedition away –'

'But they didn't and they never will. The only shots we'll hear are the ones I'll fire when we have another duck-shoot in West Angle Bay.'

It was the end of the afternoon watch and Mr Fitton had come up to take over the deck. The breeze had moderated and the cutter was making six or seven knots; the sky was clear and blue above her arching sails and under the weather-rail for'ard the men of the watch-on-deck were lounging somnolently in the sunshine. It was this pleasure-cruise atmosphere that had prompted Barrington's grumble.

'Ah well,' he said now, turning from the after rail with a quick glance aloft, 'she's yours, Mr Fitton. Keep her as she goes. And send a hand to the masthead, if you please. If dead-reckoning's anything to go by we should raise the land any moment.'

'Aye aye, sir.'

Barrington went below. Mr Fitton, after hailing Kenyon from the deck-watch to go to the masthead and checking the course on the binnacle-compass, took a meditative turn or two on the after-deck. Perhaps subconsciously, he had avoided all thought of Simone de Callac and the pigeon message for nearly twenty-four hours; Barrington's mention of the abortive Irish raid had brought it to mind again.

Légion Noire NVP. Except for the hinted involvement with Colonel Tate, it conveyed no more to him than it had done at first. The capital letters might be assumed to stand for words, an agreed code, he thought. If his previous assumptions were taken as facts the message should have reported the disruption of the invasion plan at Cork; but it could as reasonably be a warning that a supporting expedition from France was not to start. 'Do not come', it would say – *ne venez pas* – and there was *NVP* explained. And the full message –

Mr Fitton halted in his pacing and shook his head sadly. He should have grasped this before now. A Black Legion, possibly to Colonel Tate's design, was to have sailed from France to join with a force from Ireland. Where would that junction have been made? At sea, probably; possibly midway between Cork and the Bristol Channel. Where the joint force would have landed was matter for guesswork. And now there would be no landing, for though the Black Legion received no warning and duly sailed they would find no supporting fleet at the rendezvous and would turn back, as the earlier expedition had done in December. There was also the possibility that more pigeons than one had been dispatched with that same message. Simone de Callac (he admitted her to his thoughts reluctantly) would have done her best to ensure its arrival.

At this point in his reflections the expected hail came from Kenyon at the masthead, and Mr Fitton, calling him down, climbed the shrouds himself to survey *Curlew*'s landfall. An undulant ribbon of gold made a new horizon ahead, lying along the pale-blue rim of the sea. Its extent was short but lengthened away to northward as the land rose into sight, until he could see that in this direction it appeared to terminate in a bold headland. His glass and a recent study of the chart confirmed that this was Strumble Head, on the north coast of Pembrokeshire. The head was fine on the larboard bow, so wind and tide had set them a little north of their dead-reckoning course; St David's Head was a dozen miles south-west from Strumble. Still, it was no bad landfall.

Barrington was on deck and hailing him to know the news. He shouted back reassuringly and then swept his glass rightward, following the diminishing coastline until he could just discern the dim projection of St David's Head broad on the bow. Halfway along this section of the coast his glass showed him the sails of four vessels, close in to the land and just coming hull-up. Two of them were three-masters, he saw. Then Barrington's impatient shout called him down on deck, where he made his report.

'Those'll be Matthews's frigates,' Barrington said when he heard of the three-masters. 'Must have come into Cork after we left. What the deuce are they doin' on this coast?'

The Sporting Shot

'Another Irish invasion scare?' suggested Mr Fitton.

'If that's it we might see some action, Fitton. How were they bearin'?'

'Our present course will intercept them, sir.'

'We'll speak 'em, then.'

Slowly the low hills behind the Pembrokeshire coast rose as they headed in towards them, and in a few minutes the sails of the frigates and their two consorts were in sight from the cutter's deck, fine on the starboard bow and moving northward. The telescopes of both officers were focused on them as they began to come hull-up. Mr Fitton felt a touch of excitement. If Admiralty had sent two frigates to supplement their solitary 74 at Cork there must be some good reason for it. Whitehall had spies at work less equivocal than the ingenious Colonel Tate, and these might have uncovered and reported the invasion plan his own speculations had implied.

'Under main and tops'ls,' commented Barrington with his glass to his eye. 'And by God they're big 'uns – forty guns or I'm a Dutchman!'

The four vessels were fully hull-up now; a big frigate in the lead, a very large brig of 24 guns and a 12-gun lugger following, and the second frigate last in the line. They were hugging the coast so closely that seen through the lens of a telescope they appeared dangerously near to the low cliffs that rose continuously above the shore.

'Rear frigate's wearin' a commodore's broad pendant,' Barrington said. 'That's a bit of sauce, Fitton – Matthews is the senior officer on this station. We'll have to bear away a point,' he added, 'or we'll pass astern of 'em.'

The squadron was little more than a mile distant and *Curlew* was closing fast. At Barrington's order Drew, at the tiller, eased her a point to larboard, on a course that would bring her within hail of the commodore ship.

The clear golden sunlight of late afternoon lit the brown hulls with their rows of black-painted gunports and showed the colours of the Union flag at the commodore's yardarm. The leading frigate was already rounding the headland Mr Fitton had identified as Strumble Head when the cutter had approached within half a mile of the rearmost ship, her hands staring curiously from the foredeck.

'It'll be "captain to come on board" any moment now,' said Barrington as the distance lessened. 'Mr Masters! Boat ready for launching and crew to stand by!'

'She's carrying a lot of men,' Mr Fitton remarked. 'Maybe she has troops on board.'

'You're right. Deck's black with 'em. – She's backin' her foretops'l. I'd better –'

He got no further. Mr Fitton, alerted by Barrington's words, had realized that most of the men who swarmed on the frigate's deck were indeed clad in black. At the same instant he saw her gunports winking open and shouted at the top of his powerful voice.

'Mainsheet, there! Bear up, Drew – hard over!'

He sprang to assist the helmsman and together they swung the tiller over. The long boom of the mainsail swept across overhead, *Curlew* turned on her heel and spun away to starboard, and Barrington's astonished oaths were cut short by the ragged thunder of the frigate's guns.

Topmast and topsail crashed down and hung flapping, a thud and a shudder of the hull told of a hit somewhere aft. The white spouts rising from the sea astern showed that the cutter would have been smashed to matchwood had she held on her course. Now she was heading across the frigate's stern and the broadside guns, which had fired at point-blank range, would no longer bear.

Barrington was yelling orders, men were already racing up the shrouds to clear the shattered topmast.

The Sporting Shot

The frigate was drawing away but her high stern, thronged with men, was no more than a pistol-shot away from *Curlew* as she began to cross it. Mr Fitton saw a man spring from the frigate's after rail into the sea, to reappear swimming strongly towards the cutter. Barrington had seen him too.

'Ease away mainsheet! Heaving-line here, and lively!'

A musket cracked from the frigate's poop, and another shot followed it, without apparent effect on the swimmer. The distance between the two vessels was fast increasing and there was no more shooting. *Curlew*'s way was checked and the line flew straight and true, but the man who was swimming so strongly had no need of it. Mr Fitton was at the rail as he came splashing and panting to the side to be helped on board, a big man naked to the waist and wearing black breeches and stockings. It was Sam Evans.

5 Invasion

1

' 'Tis the French, sir!' Evans gasped out as soon as he found breath. 'Fourteen hundred of 'em – going to land here!'

Barrington goggled at him. 'Are they, by God! I'll have the bastards' blood, firin' on me under British colours! But how the deuce do you come to be –'

'By'r leave, sir!' called Drew from the helm. 'We're closing the shore fast!'

Curlew had come within two cable-lengths of the rocks at the foot of the coastal cliffs. Barrington ordered her to be brought to the wind, and as Drew put the helm down the boatswain came up to report the topmast wreckage cleared and down on deck.

'Very well, Mr Masters.' Barrington turned to the dripping leading seaman. 'Now, Evans. How –'

But Evans was not to tell his story for some time. Mr Tibbs came running aft, his bald head shining with sweat and his face creased with anxiety.

'Sir – sir,' he croaked breathlessly. 'We're making water by the gallon, sir – nigh on two foot over the keelson already. I can't do nothing –'

'Rig the pump, Mr Masters, and quick about it,' snapped Barrington.

'Pump won't mend it,' said the carpenter, holding his ground as the boatswain departed at a run. 'We're holed a handsbreadth below waterline, sir, and 'twas an 18-pounder ball. I can't do nothing with it 'less you can careen her.'

'*Careen!*'

'Aye, so I can come at the damage from outboard. If I don't, she'll founder, sir, sooner or later.'

Barrington pursed his lips in a soundless whistle and looked at Mr Fitton. They turned together to look along the inhospitable coast. *Curlew*'s late assailant was rounding Strumble Head and the rest of the French ships were already out of sight. They scarcely glanced at the enemy frigate; they were both seamen and at this moment the safety of their ship was more important than any threatened French invasion.

'Tide's at half ebb,' said Mr Fitton. 'No breakers and the cliffs give us a lee. If only we could find a sandy cove –'

'Carregonnen Bay!' Evans exclaimed. 'Beg pardon, sir, but that'd do us. The foreshore's rocky but there's sand at low water. Just this side of Strumble Head, sir – not half a mile away.'

Barrington hesitated, biting his lip. It meant putting his command aground on what would be a dangerous lee shore if the wind veered westerly; rendering her helpless in the presence of an enemy squadron.

'There's no alternative, sir,' Mr Fitton said quietly. 'And Evans knows this coast well,' he added.

'You're right.' Barrington turned quickly to the seaman. 'Evans, I'm trustin' you to take her in. – Drew, you'll take orders from Leading Seaman Evans. Mr Fitton, anchors ready for lettin' go fore and aft. You've materials and tackle for this repair, Mr Tibbs?'

'I have, sir. But it may take more than one tide –'

'Never mind that. Have 'em all ready. You can have as many hands as you want. For'ard, there!'

His further orders set the cutter in motion and her decks in an ordered bustle. Sail was reduced to outer jib and full-reefed mains'l, the lead was set going, gangs of men ran four of the larboard guns to the starboard rail to ensure that she settled over on that side, a hawser was rigged as a preventer stay from the larboard rail to the masthead. *Curlew*'s pump, a contraption that bolted to the rail and could only be worked by one man, was frenziedly discharging the water sucked up its canvas hose; the water was perfectly clear, a sure sign that the sea was making dangerous inroads. Slowly, with Evans watchful at Drew's side, she slanted in beneath the jagged rim of hundred-foot cliffs, nosing into the corner between the rocky bluff of Strumble Head and the northern curve of the little bay. Close on the larboard side the small waves broke on an islet of rock, and the head itself could now be seen to be an island, for a narrow cleft separated it from the turfy slopes above.

'By the mark seven,' sang the leadsman. 'And a quarter seven – quarter less seven –'

Mr Fitton, in the bows with his anchor-party, surveyed the precipitous slopes they were approaching and thought they might almost be those of some deserted Atlantic island. Above and beyond the cliffs there must be pastures and farms and some cultivation – for this was Pembrokeshire – but the coast here, utterly wild and desolate, looked as if it had never been trodden by man.

'Deep six – and a half five –'

Curlew drew three fathoms. From aft came Barrington's shout.

'Down main and jib! Let go aft! – Away boat!'

The sheet anchor plunged down from the stern. The cutter, losing what way she had, glided on until she came to by the stern and lay motionless, rocking gently on the small waves that rolled on to break on the rocks a cable-length away. The bow anchor was lowered into the boat and dropped at Mr Fitton's order halfway between ship and tide-line. *Curlew* had now to wait until the ebbing tide grounded her and she lay tilted over on the drying sand. The cliffs above, glowing in the light of the westering sun, seemed to smile benevolently; thanks to their shelter and a calm sea, a tricky operation had been safely concluded. There was time now to think of other things.

Barrington had sent Evans below to get into dry clothes and take a well-deserved double ration of rum, and was posting an anchor-watch fore and aft when Mr Fitton came up to report good holding-ground. Five minutes later the three of them were seated round the table in Barrington's cabin and Sam Evans was telling his story to two closely attentive listeners. He told it well and succinctly but with a Welshman's flair for the dramatic.

In the assault on the Perenno cliff path eight days ago he had been given no chance to strike a blow. With a thick sack rammed over head and body and his arms lashed to his sides he had been hustled up to the cliff-top and hoisted on to the back of a pony. A long and rough ride, two hours or more he thought, and then the cobbles of a street under the pony's hooves. There had been talk in French during the ride, and Colonel Tate's voice sounding assured and giving orders, so he had guessed what had happened. His captors had lugged him off the pony and hurried him into a stone building where he had been freed from sack and bonds and pushed into a great cellar-like room full of men, most of them ragged and filthy.

' 'Twas the Madeleine prison in Brest, sir,' Evans said. 'An' these was French convicts and murderers and such, come from other prisons.'

This he learned from two Irishmen, imprisoned after capture from a British regiment in Flanders. No one knew why they had been brought there. From time to time other batches of men were thrust in with them, until the big room was packed almost to suffocation.

They were fed twice a day, bread and meat and rough wine, and Sam had to fight for his meal – 'more like wild beasts than men, they was' – but this imprisonment lasted only two days. On the morning of the third day they were all herded out by French soldiers into the prison courtyard, and here they were joined by crowds of convicts brought out from other cells; more than 800 all told, as he learned later. Colonel Tate and a French naval officer in blue and gold had mounted a wooden dais and addressed the multitude in French, which one of Sam's Irish acquaintances had translated for him. They were all to have their freedom on condition that they joined the newly formed Black Legion, they would sail at once on an expedition where drink and women and plunder would be theirs for the taking, their uniforms would be issued at once. The screech of exultation that went up from the assembled criminals made Sam's blood run cold. When it had died down, the French officer's brief announcement that any man dissenting would be shot made no difference to the general elation.

'The uniforms was old 'uns dyed black,' said Sam. 'We got 'em on an' then we was marched down to the docks an' on board the ships, two 40-gun frigates an' a brig an' a lugger. Six hundred reg'lar soldiers, all in black, was embarked too. They had their muskets – ours was to be issued later on. We sailed that afternoon.'

'What day was that?' Mr Fitton asked.

Sam thought for a moment. 'Five days ago, it was. That'd make it 17 February, sir.'

So the pigeon-messenger they had shot on the 18th would have arrived too late in any case.

'And who was the damned scoundrel in command of these vessels?' demanded Barrington.

'Couldn't come by his name, sir. Far as I could make out, he commanded the ships an' Colonel Tate commanded the Black Legion, as we was called. Them two had a bust up, I reckon.'

'How was that?'

It had been yesterday morning, Sam said. The four ships had been hove-to out of sight of land for a day and a half, and the buzz on the lower deck was that they were going to attack the port of Bristol. Then the French commodore's boat had brought him on board the frigate that carried Colonel Tate.

'Me an' a few hundred others was in that ship,' Sam went on. 'One o' the Irish officers was in charge of us an' a right plaguy job he had of it.'

'Irish?' said Barrington, frowning.

'Aye, sir. There was three of 'em, two captains an' a lieutenant. Young harum-scarum lads in the French service. Our ship was sailin' last in line. We was packed below decks like herrings in a box, but we was allowed on deck fifty at a time for a breath of air. I was on deck when Tate an' the commodore was on the quarterdeck wavin' their arms an' gabblin' at one another like a pair of angry old dames. I dunno what 'twas about but after a bit the commodore pulls back to his ship an' we gets under way headin' north.'

Now that his speculations were being confirmed Mr Fitton could put a credible interpretation on this. There had been no supporting fleet at the rendezvous and the naval commander had wanted to abandon the project and return to France; Tate was the more likely of the two to propose a landing on the Pembroke coast as an alternative, and he had won the day.

' 'Twas two bells of the forenoon watch today,' Sam was saying, 'when I was brung up an' taken to the cabin. The colonel was there, smilin' friendly like. "Sam Evans", says he, "you're here to act as my pilot an' guide. Serve me faithful an' I'll see you rewarded. Play me false", says he, starin' at me very hard, "an' I'll see Gwennie Jones suffers for it". ' Sam stopped and looked from one to the other of his hearers. 'Now how could he have known about Gwennie?'

'He could only have learned about her from Simone de Callac,' said Mr Fitton, incautiously speaking his thought aloud.

'What's this?' Barrington demanded sharply. 'Who's Simone de Callac, Fitton?'

Mr Fitton had no alternative but to tell of his visit to Long Warren, the pigeons, and his deductions, which he did as briefly as possible.

'Then this woman's a spy, by God – a French agent!' Barrington exclaimed.

'So it appears. May I suggest, sir,' Mr Fitton went on quickly, 'that we allow Evans to finish his story?'

Barrington frowned and then nodded. 'Carry on, Evans.'

'Well, sir,' Sam resumed. 'I was in a cleft stick, like. But I reckoned to go along with him an' lead him astray if I could. He says he's goin' to land at Fishguard an' march across Wales pickin' up hundreds of rebel Welshmen on the way. He says he's goin' to attack Chester.'

'Chester!' Barrington exploded. 'The damned feller must be mad!'

Sam turned to him quickly. 'He's mad right enough, sir, an' murderin' mad too. Anyways, I tells him he'll have trouble at Fishguard where there's a big fort with a dozen 18-pounders above the harbour.'

'Is that true?'

'No, sir – 'tis a little old fort with eight 9-pounders. I was there on leave three months ago an' the tale was the guns hadn't been fired for four years an' there was no powder or shot for 'em. There's the Fishguard Fencibles – volunteer farm lads, most of 'em – an' they might raise as many as a hundred from round Fishguard. But that'd take time. I couldn't stop him landin', sir, but I reckoned if I could delay him I'd be doin' the right thing. So I tells him the only safe place to land is Carregwastad Point.'

'Where's that?'

'Three mile east along the Pencaer coast from Strumble. 'Tis called Pencaer, sir, this part o' the country.'

Barrington took a chart from the rack and spread it on the table. 'Show us.'

Sam's forefinger slowly traced the indented outline on the chart. Strumble Head was the apex of a right angle, the coast south of it running north-south and on its other side east-west to the deep inlet of Fishguard Bay. The moving finger stopped on a small projecting point less than two miles from the opening of the bay.

'That's it, sir,' Sam said. 'Cliffs on two sides, steep as a roof on t'other. If the colonel can get fourteen hundred men an' forty-seven barrels of powder up Carregwastad before nightfall he's a wonder.'

'He was goin' to take your advice, then?'

'Aye, sir. When we sighted Strumble Head he made me stand on the quarterdeck with him. I was to pilot him to Carregwastad, d'ye see. You can lay to it as I'd have cut an' run for it soon as I was ashore.' Sam grinned. 'It was jump an' swim for it, as it happened. Soon as I saw 'twas *Curlew* —'

He stopped suddenly. The cabin deck had jerked and shuddered under them.

'She's settlin',' Barrington said, shifting uneasily in his chair; he looked at Evans. 'Sure we're clear of rocks?'

'Take me davy on it, sir,' returned the seaman cheerfully. 'Naught but sand an' shell this far out.'

The cutter thumped bottom again, more gently. Masters's voice sounded from on deck, where the hands were making all fast.

'There's less than two hours of daylight left,' said Barrington, frowning. 'Tibbs says he can plug the hole temporarily but he'll need more time to make her seaworthy. That means we can't sail before tomorrow noon. And *Polyphemus* ought to have the news of this God-damned Black Legion right away.'

Curlew was lying motionless now except for a slight roll as the waves passed her. Her keel was resting on the bottom. Mr Fitton spoke after a pause.

'It seems to me that Tate must have decided to land at Fishguard before this expedition set sail. That explains why Evans was kidnapped – to act as guide. Now he's lost Evans.' He turned to the seaman. 'Will he find Carregwastad Point without your help?'

'He made me show him on the chart, sir. He'll land, right enough. Naught'll stop him. He's like –' Sam paused to find a simile – 'like a bull at a gate.'

'How are these fellers armed?' asked Barrington.

'Muskets an' bayonets, sir. They was to be given out afore we landed.'

Barrington looked doubtfully at his second-in-command. 'I suppose I could have at 'em with a landing party –'

'No,' Mr Fitton cut in firmly. 'You can't leave *Curlew* as she is and you'll need the hands when she sails tomorrow. We have to find where the Black Legion has landed and then – as quickly as we can – alert what forces there may be ashore here. Evans and I –'

He checked himself abruptly. This was no way to address a senior officer.

'I would suggest, sir, that you put myself and Leading Seaman Evans ashore as soon as possible, with orders to make a reconnaissance and report our findings to the military authorities.'

'If there are any,' Barrington said with a faint grin; he pondered a moment. 'Very well, Mr Fitton. I don't see what else I can do. Evans, you know this countryside, I believe.'

'Pencaer, sir? Like the back o' me hand.'

'Well, see Mr Fitton don't get lost. You can get him up these cliffs, I suppose?'

'Aye, sir – easy. I've been up an' down a score o' times.'

'And you'll report on board, Mr Fitton, as soon as your mission's completed.'

'Aye aye, sir.' Mr Fitton hesitated. 'There's no saying how long it will take. If *Curlew*'s seaworthy tomorrow afternoon what shall you do with her?'

'Sail as soon as she floats, dodge the French, and bring her into Fishguard harbour. But Gad's me life! You'll be aboard long before then.' Barrington pushed back his chair. 'We're wastin' time and you'll need a boat – 'nother half-hour and you'd be walkin' ashore.'

'I suspect I'll get all the walking I want without that,' said Mr Fitton.

2

Halfway up the steep of rock and turf that rose above Carregonnen Bay Mr Fitton halted to get his breath. Evans, a few yards ahead of him, halted also. Below them, the boulder-strewn shore and the sands newly revealed by the ebbing tide shone red-gold in the light of the setting sun, and the cutter, a hundred yards out on the glittering water, was clear in every detail. Already she was listed well over to starboard, and as they watched the small black figures of men were clambering overboard with a ladder and splashing about in the shallow water. Mr Tibbs and his repair party were wasting no time.

'Five minutes to the top, sir,' said Sam.

'Lead on, then.'

They were following a vestigial path that dodged upward avoiding the small crags that broke the slope here and there, steep but easy enough going. After a brief discussion it had been decided not to carry arms; they were not proposing to encounter the enemy and cutlass or pistol would only impede fast walking. Mr Fitton had his (or rather Barrington's) glass in his capacious side-pocket and both he and Sam carried some bread and dried meat – they had not stayed to eat before leaving *Curlew*. Close on their left now rose the flat top of Strumble Head, with gulls wheeling and crying round its fringing cliffs. Toiling up a last rise of shaly ground tufted with heather they rounded a shoulder of hill and saw the coast behind the head trending sharply eastward, though their view was limited by a heathery hump a quarter of a mile ahead.

'We'll see Carregwastad from up yonder,' Sam, said, striding on.

Far down on their left as they skirted the broken slope the waves murmured in a shadowy cove, but the spaces beyond were dazzlingly coloured. The sun was on the point of setting, its dying flames spreading across a sea barred with turquoise and green, and when they gained the summit of the hump they saw the indented cliffs of Pencaer strung like a chain of rubies along the edge of the land. The cliffs stretched away to end in a rocky headland two miles distant, beyond which the line of the far coast north of the invisible Fishguard Bay could just be discerned. Lying motionless off the headland were the four vessels of the French squadron.

'*Myn diawl*!' Sam's oath was emphatic. 'They're landin' now – see the boats, sir!'

The sea between ships and land was dotted with moving black specks. Using his glass, Mr Fitton counted eight boats, some moving landward and others heading back to the ships. He shifted the telescope a trifle to the right, focusing it on the headland of Carregwastad. The seaward face of the point was aglow with sunset colour and showed its inaccessible cliff. The inlet below its near side was hidden below an intervening rise, but the slope rising from the inlet was in full view, with a black streak slanting up its steep of turf and boulders to the neck of the headland above. It was a moment or two before he realized that the black streak was a crowd of climbing men. A thin grey column of smoke rising from the flat saddle behind the point showed where they were establishing themselves.

Mr Fitton was conscious of a sudden surge of unwonted emotion. It was anger. Britain's coast had been inviolate for centuries, secured from invasion by her navy, and now the French had landed, slipping easily and unopposed through inadequate defences. It made little difference that the invasion force was small and its objectives unimportant; the French were on British soil.

'Didn't we ought to lie down, sir?' Sam said. 'They'll easy see us up here.'

'If they do it makes no odds.'

As he spoke he realized that the converse was true also. The French had no need for concealment. Colonel Tate would have learned from Simone de Callac that there was no force to oppose the Black Legion within many miles of Fishguard; the nearest garrison was at Pembroke, which must be forty or fifty miles away. Mr Fitton used his glass to scan the countryside inland from Carregwastad Point. The sun had set, but the fading glow lit a wilderness apparently devoid of human habitation, a long shelf of thicket and swamp rising gently to the crest of low hills.

'Are there no farms hereabout?' he demanded.

'Aye, there's half-a-dozen farms, sheep an' cattle, an' a smallholdin' or two, wide apart – Pencaer's poor farmin' country, as you see. Most of the folks live round about Fishguard. But *esgob mawr!*' Sam pulled himself up short. 'I'd forgot Trehowel. That's John Mortimer's farm, sir, in the trees up yonder an' a mile or less from Carregwastad. If those black devils get at Trehowel –'

'If they do they'll find the house empty,' Mr Fitton broke in. 'Fourteen hundred men can't be landed without a deal of noise and shouting and they're lighting fires besides. Unless Mr Mortimer's deaf and blind he'll have himself and his household on the way to Fishguard by now.'

'Hope you're right, sir. Maybe they'll do the same at Llanwnda.'

'What's that? Another farm?'

'Two or three cottages an' a little church, sir, on the hill above Fishguard Bay.'

The ruddy light was fast fading over land and sea. The distant boats still plied between ships and shore and several more fires had been lit behind the headland. Mr Fitton thought fast. When he had got all his force ashore Tate had still to bring some sort of order to 1,400 men, more than half of them undisciplined; he would hardly try to move his small army across unknown country in the darkness. It was more than likely that the Black Legion would encamp where they were until daylight.

'You spoke of some volunteers at Fishguard, Sam,' he said quickly.

'Aye, sir. The Fishguard Fencibles they call 'em.'

'Who commands them?'

Sam scratched his head. 'Last time I was here I was told but damned if I can – got it! Mr Thomas Knox, he's the militia colonel.'

The name woke a memory of the fireside at Long Warren and the Comtesse de Callac enumerating her friendly neighbours.

'Colonel Knox of Minwere Lodge,' he said. 'Where's that?'

'Away down south, sir, by Haverfordwest. A long twenty mile from here.'

Twenty miles! Five or six hours on foot.

'An' Lord Cawdor as commands the Pembrokeshire Yeomenry,' Sam added, 'he's farther still, t'other side Pembroke.'

'No one of authority nearer?'

Sam thought a moment. 'There's him they call the

governor of Fishguard Fort, old Gwynne Vaughan, but he's no manner of use. Knox is the man you want, sir. He'll have hosses to carry messages –' He stopped and slapped his thigh. 'By hooky! It's hosses we need, an' we might get 'em at Tresinwen. That's Hugh Morris's farm, sir, inland from Strumble. Hugh used to breed ponies when I was a lad – many a one I've rode bareback –'

'How far from here?'

'Half-hour, sir, an' it's rough goin'.'

Mr Fitton rammed his glass into his pocket and threw a last glance at Carregwastad Point. On the water the boats were steadily at work and on land the red sparks of half-a-dozen fires winked distantly across the darkening slopes.

'Shape a course for Tresinwen, Sam, with all the sail we can carry,' he said.

'Aye aye, sir.'

Sam turned at once and started back by the way they had come. At the foot of the heathery hump he turned to the left on a narrow path that seemed to have been made by sheep or goats, announcing over his shoulder that this was a short cut he had used years ago. Mr Fitton would have said it had never been used since. It plunged through tall gorse-bushes, wound between obstructing brambles, and crossed reedy glens where their feet sank deep in the bog. Floundering blindly after his leader, he gave his thoughts to the Black Legion.

For all its apparent rashness Colonel Tate's expedition had some hope of success. If he could move his men at dawn and get past Fishguard unscathed he might well lose all pursuit in the desolate river valleys and hills to northward. So far as Mr Fitton could remember there were no towns of any importance for a hundred miles in that direction; which meant that there would be no armed forces to oppose a small army of desperadoes 1,400 strong. In a country where communications were so difficult and distances to the nearest military centres so great he might well burn and pillage his way as far as Chester. Of course he would be caught in the end, but the damage he would do to the country's confidence in its invulnerability – not to speak of the trail of rape and murder he would leave behind him – would be enormous. He must be halted at Fishguard. And the only armed men who could do it were amateur soldiers, scattered across a county. It would take many hours, perhaps days, to muster them. The man who could order that had to be found and alerted as quickly as possible.

With this consciousness of the shortness of time gaining upon him, he strode and stumbled in Sam Evans's wake, holding with difficulty to the fast pace the seaman was setting. The way trended always uphill and the fast-falling twilight made the path through the thickets difficult to see. Twice Sam took a wrong opening in the bushes and had to retrace a step or two. Overhead the evening sky was cloudless and a few stars winked palely, and in the scarcely cool air of this phenomenal February weather Mr Fitton sweated mightily as he pounded on. There would be a half-moon later, he remembered; that would be useful if he was to ride twenty miles or more in darkness – or walk it, for there was no certainty of finding mounts at Tresinwen. It could be midnight before they reached Minwere Lodge.

They were on open hillside now and free of bogs and thickets. Beyond a stone wall on their right a flock of sheep, a pale amorphous cloud in the gloaming, drifted down a field. A low ridge of rock rose black against the evening sky ahead, and as he saw it Mr Fitton heard the *clop-clop* of a horse's hooves receding on the farther side of the ridge. Sam led away to the left where the ridge dipped in a gap closed by a gate, which they passed through to a sudden outburst of barking, and steered a route across a cobbled yard to the farmhouse whose lamplit window glimmered below a sheltering cliff. Light spilled across the cobbles as the door was opened and a man's voice screeched an order that instantly quelled the noise of the dogs. A moment later a short bearded Welshman was grasping Sam's hand with an astonished shout of welcome.

For the next few minutes Mr Fitton could only stand and listen to two voices talking excitedly in rapid Welsh. Then Sam swung round to face him.

' 'Tis bad news an' good, sir,' he said swiftly. 'Hugh here sold all his ponies afore Christmas. The only beast he's got is a cart-horse, an' likely he'll need that for cartin' his goods clear of the French. But –'

'I heard a horse leaving here as we approached,' Mr Fitton interposed.

'Aye, sir. 'Twas Owen from the mill down by Tregwynt. He'd been payin' a call here and bringin' the gossip – an' that's the good news, sir. Colonel Knox is at Tregwynt, which is down the road four mile. Seems Mrs Harries of Tregwynt –'

'Tell me as we go.'

Mr Fitton swung on his heel, Sam called a farewell in Welsh to Hugh Morris, and they hurried out of the yard.

The sky overhead was like green glass spangled with stars, and gave light for their footing on the rough track beyond the farm. As they went Sam talked. Tregwynt was a big old house belonging to Mrs Harries, a wealthy widow, who had chosen this night to give a ball. The gentry from across the county would be here, Colonel Knox among them.

'Is that certain?' Mr Fitton demanded.

'Aye, sir. Owen the mill was watchin' from the stables an' saw him ride in with his groom ridin' after him. 'Tis a rare stroke o' luck for us,' Sam added, 'but not so lucky for Colonel Knox – he'll miss his dance.'

They left the track through a gate and were on a lane between hedges, running uphill. Fast though they were walking, Sam had breath enough to go on talking. Hugh Morris, he said, had been scared at the news of the French landing; he proposed to harness his wagon and take himself and his family to a friend's farm farther inland.

'I would have thought Tresinwen safe enough from Tate's men,' Mr Fitton said.

'If he lets them cut-throats loose there's no farm or cottage 'll be safe from 'em,' Sam said positively. 'An' there's more to it than that. There was a wreck –'

A fortnight ago, so Morris had told him, a smuggling brig with a full cargo had been wrecked south of Strumble Head. Casks of rum and brandy by the score had been washed ashore and were now stored in the cellars or kitchens of every dwelling in the neighbourhood.

'If the Black Legion gets its claws on drink there'll be the devil to pay an' no pitch hot,' Sam ended.

Mr Fitton said nothing, but the need for haste nagged at him more urgently. He tried to lengthen his stride to match the seaman's longer legs.

The lane ran almost straight between low banks topped by leafless hedges. So far as he could see in the starlight it passed no dwellings until, after a silent half-hour of walking at top speed, it swooped steeply down into a narrow glen and crossed a stream by a stone bridge. In the glen below the bridge was a building with a lit window; that must be Owen's mill. The short steep hill out of the glen tried his leg muscles sorely, but at the top the lane widened and levelled and there was the gleam of many lights through the trees on their right.

'Tregwynt,' Sam said.

Without slackening their pace they swung in between the pillars of an imposing gateway and up a broad gravelled drive. The big two-storeyed house they were approaching had all its lower windows ashine. The light of the lantern above its big porch glinted on the paintwork of four or five carriages that stood to one side of it, and from the stables and outbuildings beyond them sounded the stamp and snuffle of horses and the muted chatter of servants' voices. Mr Fitton strode up to the porch door and tugged at the iron-handled bell-pull. His glance took in the manservant who opened the door but passed beyond him.

A large hallway, a log fire blazing in a big fireplace; at its farther end an open door through which men and women were passing into the brilliantly lit room beyond. The last couple, a tall man in a blue uniform and a woman in a dress of grey silk, were just leaving the hall. The woman was Simone de Callac.

3

It took Mr Fitton a moment only to perceive that he might have expected this; an *émigrée* Comtesse living less than ten miles away would be sure to be invited to Mrs Harries's ball. But the shock of seeing her had checked his utterance and the manservant spoke first.

'Well? What may *you* want?'

The man's tone made him conscious of his torn white breeches, his muddy blue coat and the plaster on the side of his head. He spoke more loudly in consequence.

'Find Colonel Knox. I've urgent news for him.'

The tall man by the far door had heard him. He closed the door on his companion and came across the hall with hasty strides.

'What's this, Jenkins?' He looked down his long nose at Mr Fitton. 'I am Colonel Knox, my man. Who the devil are you?'

'Fitton, master's mate in His Majesty's armed cutter *Curlew*.' He took off his hat and walked in without waiting for an invitation. 'The French are landing on Carregwastad Point, sir. They number fourteen hundred and there are four French warships lying off the point.'

Colonel Knox stared at him with dropped jaw and goggling eyes. He was a youngish man with a thin high-coloured face and brown hair elaborately curled. His blue uniform coat had yellow facings and there was lace at his throat and wrists.

'That's damned nonsense!' he said sharply at last. 'I don't believe it. Those ships are not French.'

'It's true nevertheless.' Mr Fitton beckoned to Sam, who had been waiting modestly in the porch. 'Leading seaman Evans will confirm what I say. Two hours ago we saw –'

'Wait,' snapped Knox. 'Jenkins, ask Colonel Vaughan to be good enough to join us.'

'We saw the actual landing in progress,' pursued Mr Fitton firmly as the servant hurried away. 'There are four hundred regulars and eight hundred enlisted convicts, calling themselves the Black Legion. They are commanded by an American, Colonel Tate.'

Knox snorted contemptuously. 'Fiddlesticks! How the devil can you know all this?'

'Evans here was captured by the French and escaped. It's thanks to him we have this information.'

'I don't believe it – I can't believe it. They'd never dare to land. And at Carregwastad, of all the unlikely places – Daniel! Come and hear this.'

A short, stout old man with grey hair and a red face was limping across the hall with the aid of a stick. He wore a uniform like Knox's; Mr Fitton thought it was probably the uniform of the Fishguard Fencibles.

'How now, Tom!' he puffed as he came up to them; his keen little eyes surveyed the visitors. 'What have we here? Two Navy men?'

'So they say,' Knox said. 'Daniel, this fellow says the

ships you saw this afternoon are French warships.'

'I didn't see 'em. My man Gwilym was out on the cliffs with the dogs and saw 'em. He told me they were brigs and a brace of sloops out of Milford.'

'He says they're landing fourteen hundred men on Carregwastad Point. He says his name is Fitton and he's a master's mate.'

'Carregwastad! That's the last place anyone would land.'

'That's what I say!' Knox cried. 'The whole damned tale won't bear belief.'

'Master's mate.' Colonel Vaughan fixed a penetrating stare on Mr Fitton. 'What ship?'

'*Curlew*, armed cutter. And I suggest, sir –'

'Captain?'

'Lieutenant Beaufort Barrington.'

'Barrington!' Vaughan looked at Knox. 'That's Howe's grand-nevvy. This officer of his may know what he's talking about.'

'I know two 40-gun frigates when I see them,' Mr Fitton said with some acerbity. 'And I'm not accustomed to having my word doubted. I tell you again that fourteen hundred French soldiers are being landed on Carregwastad Point at this moment. I suggest you lose no time in acting against them.'

Knox reddened. 'You expect us to believe this –'

'Wait, Tom,' the older man broke in. 'Let's hear this tale of yours, Mr Fitton. Then we'll see about acting.'

Restraining his impatience, Mr Fitton complied as briefly as he could, omitting all but the essentials. When he had finished he turned to Sam Evans, who was standing at his shoulder.

'Evans will confirm that what I've said is true.'

'True as gospel, sir,' Sam answered. 'By 'r leave, sir, you didn't tell these gentlemen as how Colonel Tate means to march on Chester.'

'Chester!' Knox shouted the word incredulously.

'That caps all! No one but a damned madman would propose such a thing!'

'That's beside the point, Tom,' Vaughan said sharply. 'Mr Fitton's story will hold water, to my mind. I don't doubt the French are landing.'

'I'll believe it when I see it,' Knox said stubbornly.

'Then for God's sake go and see it, man!' snapped Vaughan impatiently, striking his stick on the floor. 'Garnfolch overlooks Trehowel and Carregwastad, and you can ride there in twenty minutes.'

Knox gnawed his lip and glanced irresolutely at the door at the end of the hall. 'What about – Meg Harries and her guests?'

'Break up the party. Home with 'em. Except the men who can ride. I'll see to all that.'

'But we don't know yet whether –'

'I'm treating this as an emergency, Colonel Knox!' Vaughan said, glaring at him. 'I believe I've more experience than you?'

Knox looked as if he would have liked to contest the point, but contented himself with an answering glare. 'Very well. Jenkins! To the stables and tell Morgan to saddle both horses – stay!' He glanced at Mr Fitton. 'You can ride, I suppose?'

'I can. So can Evans.'

'You'll ride with me. Evans can wait in the kitchen. Jenkins, Morgan is to saddle Mrs Harries's pony as well – and tell him to hurry.'

Five minutes later Mr Fitton, astride Mrs Harries's pony, was trotting out of Tregwynt gateway in the wake of Colonel Knox and his groom Morgan. His natural resentment at Knox's doubt of his news was lost in exasperation at this wasting of critical time. It was no good telling himself that his part in the matter of the Black Legion's landing ended with the delivery of the news to the shore authorities; he felt, as he had felt from the start, that fortune (or his Tutelary Genius) had involved him personally with Colonel Tate and his wild ambitions. His plain duty, he reflected as they jogged uncomfortably down the first steep hill, had been to decline to put himself under Knox's orders; his captain had ordered him to return on board when his mission was completed. If the shore authorities seemed slow and incompetent, it was not for a master's mate to interfere. All the same, he could not bring himself to return to *Curlew*, stranded in her lonely bay on the wrong side of Strumble Head, while an invasion was taking place farther along the coast. He could not leave such a kettle of fish when it was just coming to the boil.

Fortunately – for he was not a good horseman – Mrs Harries's pony was a docile animal. It was not a fast goer, however. The colonel and his groom both rode hunters, and when they had crossed the stone bridge in the glen and were breasting the hill above it the pony fell behind. On the long straight lane beyond Knox maintained a fast trot, and by urging his beast to a canter Mr Fitton could follow at a hundred yards' distance. The half-moon had risen above the dark humps and hollows on their right and the Pencaer countryside lay peaceful under a windless sky, silent except for the clatter of their horses' hooves. A man might be forgiven, he thought, for doubting that an invading army lay not five miles away, behind the long hill-crest that rose ahead and hid the coast and sea beyond.

They passed the entrance to the Tresinwen lane, and he perceived now that the hill-crest was the higher continuation of the ridge he and Sam had crossed earlier that night. Two cottages stood by the lane a little farther on, and from the lamplit doorway of one of them a man shouted to ask if they had heard the news. Knox rode on without a word and in another half-mile led off up a cart-track on the left. It was steep and rough and soon gave out on open hillside even steeper, where the ground rose in shelves and protruding boulders. Here they dismounted. Leaving Morgan in charge of their mounts, Knox and Mr Fitton, the colonel leading the way, clambered on up the turfy ledges.

There was a faint wind up here and Mr Fitton could smell the sea. One or two sheep started up from nooks in the rocks and went plunging away. Then he was aware of black shapes overhead against the night sky and a moment later was standing beside a cluster of huge boulders on the summit. The prospect on the farther side lay spread before them.

'Good God!' exclaimed Knox, and relapsed into a stricken silence.

The spaces beneath them embraced a wide stretch of land and sea, but whereas the distant sea was a plain of darkness the land was coruscating with ruddy light. Close-set and filling a square mile or more were scores of fires. Round each of them there was ceaseless movement, though the figures of men were too far away to be distinguished. Even at this distance – Mr Fitton guessed it to be a mile and a half – the hum of many hundreds of voices came to their ears like the murmur of a great city.

'See there – beyond the fires!' Knox said suddenly. 'The scoundrels have fired a barn!'

Mr Fitton had his glass to his eye. 'No, sir,' he said. 'They're still bringing stuff ashore and they've set the gorse afire to light their way.' He handed the glass over. 'Look beyond that blaze and you'll just make out the four ships lying off.'

'You're right, by God! The damned impudent dogs!'

'And I believe you owe me an apology, colonel,' Mr Fitton added evenly.

'Eh?' Knox sounded startled. 'Oh, ah – well, you have it, Mr – um – Fitton. But who'd have thought – fourteen hundred, did you say?'

'Yes. More than half of them undisciplined jail-birds.'

'My God! If we can raise four hundred militia we'll be fortunate – and that can't be done in less than twenty-four hours!'

'It can be attempted, sir,' Mr Fitton said quickly. 'The sooner your messengers are away –'

'Come on!'

Knox thrust the telescope at him and started down the slope at breakneck speed. When they reached the horses he sprang into the saddle and was off like the wind, with his groom pounding after him down the steep track. Mr Fitton on his pony was already far behind when the horses turned into the lane and set off at a gallop; and since the pony seemed unwilling or unable to do more than canter he resigned himself to being left behind. There was after all no need for hurry on his part. Colonel Knox, that doubting Thomas, was quick enough to act once he was convinced.

The two wayside cottages they had passed were unlit and deserted-looking when he came to them. Probably the inhabitants had made for Fishguard – this lane must lead down to Fishguard Bay in two or three miles, and Fishguard was the only centre for this widespread community, the natural gathering-place for folk in perplexity or fear. The little town must be well aware of the danger by now, even though Tate's activities on Carregwastad were out of sight from it; the glow in the sky from the fires would confirm the news brought in by the fugitives from the farms.

As the dark hedges unreeled on either hand and the moonlit lane sped behind under his pony's hooves, he turned his thoughts to *Curlew*. Tucked away beneath those sheltering cliffs of the wild north-west coast she should be safe enough from discovery by the French. They had no need to patrol the coast, and all Tate's attention would be fixed on the Fishguard front of his troops. All the same, any chance discovery would find her helpless, at the enemy's mercy; and in any such danger his place was on board his ship. He resolved to get himself and Evans back to her as soon as possible.

The pony was breasting the last steep rise to the gates of Tregwynt when a horseman clattered out of the gateway and galloped away along the lane heading southward. In the courtyard was a bustle of men and lanterns and horses; all the carriages had gone. Evidently old Colonel Vaughan had not wasted the hour of Knox's absence, and it looked as though Knox – who must have returned only ten minutes ago – was wasting no time either. As Mr Fitton rode up to the open doorway of the house and dismounted, a stableman came running and took away the pony, and a moment later he turned to find Sam Evans at his side.

'I thought you might be glad o' this, sir,' Sam said. 'I've had my fill in the kitchen.'

He held out a brimming pewter tankard of ale. Mr Fitton thanked him heartily and swallowed its contents before he spoke again.

'We're heading back to *Curlew*, Sam,' he said. 'Stand by for me in the porch here.'

He stepped into the hall. There were only three men in it: Knox was writing furiously at a small table while a young man, booted and spurred, stood waiting; old Vaughan was across the room from Knox, studying a map that had been tacked to the oak panelling. Vaughan beckoned to him as he came in.

'We're acting on your information as quickly as possible, Mr Fitton,' he said, 'as you'll no doubt be glad to know. Riders have already set off to Lord Cawdor for the Castlemartin Yeomanry – that's fifty men – and to Major Bowen and Lord Milford. There are the Volunteers at Fishguard and at Newport too.'

'How many all told, sir?'

'If we're fortunate, maybe five hundred men by tomorrow nightfall.'

'Little more than a third of the French numbers,' Mr

Fitton commented.

'Aye – but in two days we can bring in the militia from Cardigan and Carmarthen and farther afield, two thousand and more.'

'If Tate doesn't delay his advance, they will be too late, sir.'

'Too late indeed. So our task is to hold 'em if we can. See here.' Vaughan, leaning on his stick, set a gnarled forefinger on the map. 'This fellow Tate can't move his damned army anywhere without passing Fishguard. If he's got any military sense at all, he'll have outposts on Goodwick Hill – here – looking across the bay to the town and harbour a mile and more away. If we can make a show of strength there we may check his advance, d'ye see.'

Mr Fitton saw all too plainly that if Colonel Tate chose to advance on Fishguard tomorrow morning he would find only a few score armed men to oppose him. But he forbore to comment; his concern now was to return to his ship. He was about to say so when he was interrupted by Knox, who crossed the hall to them.

'That's the last away,' Knox said; a diminishing clatter of hooves confirmed his words. 'I think we've done all we can, Daniel. I'll ride for Fishguard at once. You'll stay here?'

The old man nodded. 'Aye. I packed Meg Harries and her maid off in the Colbys' carriage, so there's myself and Jenkins and the stablemen. We'll barricade the house. I'll post a man at the head of the lane as sentinel –'

'By God!' Knox dashed fist into palm. 'I should have posted a man on Garnfolch to keep observation on the enemy – I should have left you there, Fitton.'

'You'd make a damned poor general, Tom,' Vaughan observed. 'But it's easy remedied. Mr Fitton goes back to Garnfolch now, his man with him, and –'

'Your pardon, sir,' Mr Fitton cut in firmly, 'but I've

my captain's order to return on board as soon as my news was delivered.'

'But damn it, man!' Knox blustered. 'There's no one left responsible enough. If your captain were here he'd change your orders when he knew –'

'He's not here, Colonel Knox, and my orders stand.'

Knox flushed angrily. 'Devil take your impudence! My orders are paramount here! You'll obey them or I'll see you –'

'Wait, wait, wait!' Vaughan interrupted loudly. 'No cause for this. Mr Fitton, you see our need, surely.' He turned to Knox. 'I propose a compromise, Tom. Garnfolch's not a mile out of Fitton's way back to Carregonnen Bay. He and the seaman go up there – see what's happening in the French camp. Evans knows the country. He reports to you at Fishguard. If Fitton's satisfied that the French aren't moving, he goes on down to his ship. That do?'

Knox fingered his chin irresolutely. 'I suppose it'll have to do,' he said sullenly after a moment. 'Very well. I can't delay longer. Fitton, my headquarters will be the Royal Oak tavern in Fishguard. Your man will report to me there.'

He turned and hurried out through the porch. Colonel Vaughan shot an apologetic glance at Mr Fitton.

'I doubt it should be requests, not orders, from one service to another,' he said.

It had been on the tip of Mr Fitton's tongue to refuse the colonel's compromise, but he had decided against it. It seemed to him highly improbable that the French would make any move before morning, and an hour's delay in getting back to *Curlew* could make little difference.

'I comply with your request, sir,' he said with a faint grin.

The sound of departing hoofbeats came in through

the open door as he spoke. Vaughan snapped his fingers.

'Morgan's riding the pony,' he said quickly, 'and there's not another horse left. I fear there's a long walk before you – long for a sea-officer, that is.'

'If I were ever forced to join your service, sir,' Mr Fitton replied with gravity, 'I would prefer the infantry to the cavalry.'

Colonel Vaughan, chuckling, limped beside him to the door and bade him look out for Frenchmen. Evans was waiting, and the two of them walked past the now deserted yard and out through the gates of Tregwynt into the moonlit lane. It was the fourth time Mr Fitton had crossed the little bridge at the bottom of the hill; this four miles of lane, he reflected, was becoming somewhat over-familiar.

They were halfway up the hill beyond when another and more disturbing thought crossed his mind. Though he had had every opportunity, he had not told Colonel Thomas Knox that one of his fellow-guests at Tregwynt was a French secret agent.

6   Pencaer by Moonlight

1

The half-moon overhead in a clear sky gave light enough for Mr Fitton to read the dial of his watch. It was past two o'clock in the morning. He and Sam had trudged three miles from Tregwynt, and his old shoes, soaked in the Pencaer bogs earlier that night, were beginning to irk his feet. He thrust the watch back into his pocket and marched doggedly on beside the big seaman.

The land that lay silvered by the moon on either side of the lane seemed less peaceful and deserted than it had done when they had come this way before. It was astir. Sounds came now and then to his ears – a distant shout, the noise of cartwheels, a horse's hoofbeats – telling that the news of invasion had reached farm or cottage somewhere among the hilly fields and copses. Many of the countryfolk, not knowing whither the French might strike, would get themselves and their belongings to Fishguard and the safety – as they thought – of numbers; a few doubters or unbelievers, he supposed, would stay obstinately in their little homesteads. It would go hard with these stay-at-homes if Tate's 800 thieves and murderers escaped from his control.

In front of them now the Garnfolch ridge lifted its long crest, the big rocks on its summit clear in the moonlight. In another half-mile they passed the two deserted lane-side cottages and Mr Fitton began to look out for the cart-track that led up the Garnfolch slopes.

'If you have to bear a message from Garnfolch summit to Fishguard, Sam,' he said, 'how will you shape your course?'

'Down again to this lane, sir, an' down the lane to the bridge above Goodwick Sands. Fishguard town's less 'n a gunshot beyond – call it three mile in all. 'Twon't take me – *diawl*!'

Sam's exclamation was jerked out of him as he came to a sudden halt. Mr Fitton, too, stopped in his tracks to stare incredulously ahead. Here the lane, rounding a shoulder of hill, ran between dark leafless thickets, and a tall man in military uniform had stepped from the thickets to confront them fifty yards away. Moonlight glinted on the barrel of the musket in his hands.

Mr Fitton cursed the folly that had made him come out unarmed. And yet – this man had not the look of a Black Legionary. The white breeches showed plainly, the coat was undoubtedly red, the tall black headpiece could only be the shako of a British infantryman – a grenadier. He took a step forward.

'Stay you there, man!' the grenadier roared instantly, advancing. 'You iss my prissoners – does you comprenny me, now?'

Sam let out a sudden shout of laughter. 'By hookey!' he cried. ' 'Tis Jemima Nicholas, from Fishguard. *Shwd wy ti*, Jemima?'

They walked on to meet the apparition, Sam exchanging question and answer in rapid Welsh as they went. As soon as she was out in clear moonshine Mr Fitton saw that it was indeed a woman, albeit a woman of greater height and breadth than most men. She wore a black steeple-crowned hat, a short red cloak, and a white apron (like the women he had seen in Haverfordwest, he remembered), and in a fist like a

Pencaer by Moonlight

blacksmith's she grasped the long pitchfork he had taken for a musket. When they met, the Welsh duologue continued for some little while, allowing him time to observe that Jemima Nicholas was nearly a head taller than himself, swarthy and craggy-faced, and apparently no longer young.

'She tells me Fishguard's full o' folk gettin' away from the French, sir,' Sam said, breaking off his conversation. 'One o' them as came in was a friend o' Jemima's who saw those black devils slaughtering one o' her cows an' got away just in time. Jemima reckoned she'd come up here an' have a go at makin' 'em pay for that.' He turned to the big Welshwoman. 'This is Mr Fitton, Jemima. He's an officer of the Navy.'

Jemima planted her pitchfork firmly with one hand, gathered a fold of her skirt with the other, and dropped a curtsey. Mr Fitton lifted his hat and made a bow.

'My good – er – madam,' he began somewhat awkwardly, 'let me dissuade you from your plan of harassing the French. They're armed with musket and bayonet and will have no mercy if they take you. The militia will deal with them in due course. Meanwhile, I advise you to return to Fishguard –'

'I shall thank you, sir,' her deep voice broke in firmly, 'and I shall do what I have come here to do.'

With that, she turned on her heel, shouldered her pitchfork, and departed with long strides the way she had come. Sam shouted something after her but she strode on, to vanish into the hillside thicket.

'I never thought to meet an Amazon,' Mr Fitton remarked. 'Are there many like her about here?'

'Nay, sir, there's but the one Jemima.' Sam chuckled. 'Cobbler in Fishguard, she is, an' not a man there can stand up to her in a fight. But there's two or three hundred others as 'd fight tooth an' nail if the French came at 'em,' he added.

The cart-track mounting the lower slopes of

Garnfolch was close on their left, and they started up it.

'And do many of these other women dress as Jemima was dressed?' Mr Fitton asked when they had gone a few paces.

'All on 'em, sir. Wouldn't be seen dead without their *clogyn coch* an' their *brat*.'

Mr Fitton said no more. But in the depths of his mind the seed of a fantastic idea had been planted.

The rutted track mounted steadily, and in ten minutes they had reached the place where the horses had been left on his previous ascent of Garnfolch. Sam spoke again as they started up the steep hillside above.

'Luck!' he growled, half to himself. 'The luck's all with the Frogs in this business. 'Twas luck made 'em pick on the finest February for twenty years to come on this coast. They'd not have landed anywhere 'twixt St David's an' Dinas Head if the weather had behaved itself normal. D'ye reckon that Colonel Tate knows how lucky he's been, sir?'

Mr Fitton, who had no breath for talk, could only grunt by way of reply. But he too was considering Colonel Tate as he clambered up the shelving turf. The man was clearly rash to the point of madness but he was no fool; he must see his position as plainly as his opponents did. The alarm had been given, but he would be aware that no force sufficient to oppose his Black Legion could reach Fishguard within twenty-four hours – Simone de Callac would have told him that. So he would certainly move on Fishguard tomorrow morning, easily overcome such trifling opposition as he might find there, and – if his threats were anything to go by – sack and pillage the little town before marching north. If only he could be delayed for a day –

Mr Fitton's foot slipped on a loose rock, and he barely saved himself from rolling back down the slope. His thoughts, however, ran on without interruption. There was no possible way of delaying the Black Legion's advance. Fishguard was doomed, and a hundred farms and villages to northward of it would be ravaged before the raiding army was caught and disarmed as in the end it must be. Even if by some miracle the attack on Fishguard was held back for 36 hours there would still be only 500 men to defend it against 1,400.

The summit rocks of Garnfolch loomed above. As he clambered up the last steep ascent, with Sam close behind him, the land breeze fanned his cheek, its chill breath a reminder that February was a winter month. Two tiny sounds, like the snapping of twigs, came to his ear in quick succession.

'That's muskets!' Sam exclaimed.

They went up the last few yards of the hill slope at a rush and stood panting beside the clustered boulders. For the second time that night Mr Fitton looked down on the French encampment.

At first glance the curious spectacle spread below him seemed little changed from his first view of it. The wide galaxy of fires glowed and flamed redly between hill and sea, the hollows and thickets round them now showing as shadows in the pale moonlight. But he was immediately aware of noise and movement down there. Shouts and answering shouts, a discordant yell, something that might be men singing in harsh chorus, came faint but clear to his ears. Then another musket-shot. And in two places among the fires there was the stir of quick movement, of numbers of men in turmoil. Heedless of Sam's exclamations, he dragged the telescope from his pocket. The narrow lens was not suited for night use and the blur of smoke from the fires prevented clear observation, but he caught and held a vision of wild black figures leaping and falling round one of the fires, and by another he glimpsed a crowd of men milling round what could be a big cask. As he lowered the glass from his eye he caught sight of a yellow flame far to the left of the encampment.

'That's Tresinwen!' Sam cried angrily. ' 'Twill be the hayloft, damn their eyes – God send Hugh Morris is safe away!'

The distant rattle of musketry – a ragged volley – sounded as he spoke. A thin yelling followed it. Sam suddenly slapped his thigh.

'By hookey, they've come on the liquor! That's what 'tis, sir, or I'm a Dutchman!'

Mr Fitton had remembered the cargo of spirits that had come ashore and had reached the same conclusion. He was thinking fast. If the Black Legion's convict horde had got their hands on drink Colonel Tate was in sore trouble. There were 800 of them and they were plundering the farms beyond their camp, as the blaze at Tresinwen showed. He had a mental picture of Tate and his officers, with their 600 regular soldiers, striving to quell a drunken mutiny, with half the mutineers dispersed over a tangled countryside at night, and the rest drinking themselves into a stupor round the fires. It could be many hours before any semblance of order was restored – and when that was done it would be some time before Tate's army would be in a fit state to fight. It was already well after three in the morning; if he had planned to march on Fishguard at daybreak that plan would almost certainly have to be abandoned. Here was a gain of precious time. Knox, feverishly organizing his puny defences, must be informed of it. Should he also be told, Mr Fitton wondered, of the somewhat unlikely scheme that had come to him on the way up Garnfolch?

He recalled Vaughan's phrase – 'a show of strength'. He remembered, from a fortnight ago, how the market-place at Haverfordwest had looked like a parade-ground full of soldiers. He saw again the uniformed grenadier who had resolved himself into Jemima Nicholas. By all the Fates, it was worth trying! He made his decision and spoke at once.

'Sam, you'll make for the Royal Oak at Fishguard.

Pencaer by Moonlight

Find Colonel Knox and tell him what we've seen. Tell him that in my opinion the French attack will be delayed until noon or even later.'

'Aye aye, sir.'

'And Sam, there's a plan he might care to consider.' Mr Fitton rapidly outlined his idea of it. 'Put that to Colonel Knox as if you'd thought of it yourself. He's not fond of me.'

'I'll do that, sir,' said Sam with a chuckle.

'And if Knox thinks nothing of it see what you can do yourself. Jemima Nicholas would lend a hand, if you can find her.'

'Aye aye, sir. She might find us a few pitchforks, too. You stayin' up here, sir?'

Mr Fitton hesitated, but only for a second. He felt a strong reluctance to remove himself from the scene of these exciting developments. He would have liked, indeed, to go down to Fishguard himself and persuade Knox to adopt his plan, which seemed likely to be the British force's only hope. But he had been ordered to return to his ship and he had been away ten hours. He would hold to the resolution he had made earlier.

'I shall rejoin *Curlew* and report to Mr Barrington,' he said. 'I believe I can find my way back.'

'You'll not go by way of Tresinwen,' Sam said with finality, 'or you'll run into them murderin' Frogs. See here, sir – go straight down from here, course nor'-west as near as a toucher, rough goin' but 'tis a clear night. In ten minutes you'll see a farm below. That's Caerlem, Dick Williams's place. I'd keep clear of it one side or t'other lest the French are in it. Straight on nor'west from Caerlem, no path but easy goin', an' you'll come down to the butt o' Strumble Head where we came up from the cutter.'

'Very well.' Mr Fitton turned, and paused. 'I don't know how things will go, but Mr Barrington will try to bring *Curlew* into Fishguard. If he does, you'll report on board. Carry on, now.'

'Aye aye, sir – an' you watch out for the Frogs.'

Sam trotted away past the group of boulders and disappeared down the way they had come up. Mr Fitton went to the verge of the summit for a last look at the French encampment. The muted hubbub of contending voices was continuous, and he thought he could hear drunken singing, but there were no more musket-shots. If the volley they had heard had been an attempt to quiet the revellers it had not succeeded. That there was violent movement among the blazing fires he could be certain, but the half-moon was low in the west now and from a mile's distance it was not possible to make out details. As he turned away to begin the descent the thin notes of a bugle-call reached his ear. Perhaps Colonel Tate was mustering his regulars to search for the errant desperadoes.

2

A veil of light haze had drawn across the night sky, but the constellations shone mistily through it and there was no difficulty in shaping his nor'-westerly course. A hollow in a fold of the hillside led downward, a shoulder on his right cutting him off from sight and sound of the French encampment, and in front and below him, perhaps two miles away, he could make out the pale line of the coast fringing a boundless darkness that was the sea. It would be full tide now, and *Curlew* would be afloat. He wondered how far Mr Tibbs had got with his repair to her wounded side; it would only be a temporary remedy in any case, and the cutter would have to return to Plymouth and the dockyard to be made really seaworthy again. If Barrington could make sail in the afternoon, however, and bring her round to Fishguard Bay, her guns could be used against the French.

Pencaer by Moonlight

At this point his reflections were abruptly ended by a near escape from a headlong fall over a boulder. Though the sloping hollow was not unduly steep, its floor was broken by projecting rocks and sudden turfy declivities, and since the sinking moon was hidden by the hill ridge on his left it was in deep shadow. It was hard to tell whether a patch of blackness ten feet away was a hole in the hillside or a lump of rock. Mr Fitton recalled a dictum of Epictetus; his favourite philosopher asserted that progress in life depended on 'a right use of the appearances of things'. His progress downhill at this moment depended on that, too. He concentrated on finding safe places for putting his feet.

In ten minutes or so the hollow widened and the ground became less steep. Clumps of gorse bushes loomed like giant beasts crouching to spring, and twice he had to skirt large beds of brambles. The stars assured him that he was still holding his course, however, and he began to peer ahead for the farm Sam had told him to pass – Caerlem, Sam had called it, Dick Williams's place. At first he could see no building in the dimly lit confusion of rock and thicket and pasture that spread away towards the now invisible coast. Instead, he was suddenly confronted by a wall. It ran right across his front, five feet high and built of rocks craftily piled without the use of cement, curving slightly downhill to his right to round a rocky bluff that stood up dark against the stars. Mr Fitton had climbed such walls in his boyhood days, and he was well aware that only by daylight could such a crossing be made without a strong likelihood of ending up with a broken leg amid the ruins of the collapsed wall. Sam hadn't mentioned this obstacle, probably assuming he would come down to the gate in it which must be somewhere farther along. He went to the right along the wall and in a hundred paces found it, a five-barred farm gate secured by a hook and ring. When he had passed through it the obscuring bluff had fallen back, revealing a small farmhouse just below him. It was scarcely a musket-shot away, and he halted to consider his route.

The house and its two outbuildings lay like grey shadows in the uncertain luminescence of the dying moon. He could see no light, hear no sound; its flocks and herds, if there were any, must be in more distant fields. It was defended by a veritable maze of stone-walled enclosures, through the gaps and gates of which he would have to grope his way – and if it was occupied there would be the barking of dogs to advertise his presence. But to go back and seek a wider circuit might land him in worse difficulties. He went on.

A gap into an empty fold, a gate into another – he was being edged nearer to the farmhouse. He could see that it faced the hillside, that its doorway had a porch made by two tall flakes of rock capped by another, and that the gate of the yard surrounding the house gave on to open land slanting towards the coast. There was his way. As he stepped down to the stone slabs of the yard, he stumbled over an obstruction and bent to investigate it. It was a dead dog, killed by thrust of sword or knife.

Now with every sense alert, he began to move across the yard towards the gate. The movement brought the end of the house into his view and there was a lit window in it. Precisely as he caught sight of the window there came to his ears, from inside the house, a scream followed by a man's angry shout.

Mr Fitton's business was to get himself back to his ship as quickly as possible and without risking contact with the French, but he could not ignore that scream. It was a woman's scream, and it seemed to him to hold both pain and terror. He went quickly across the yard to the uncurtained window and peered cautiously in. Another scream came more loudly as he did so. The house wall was three feet thick and because he was looking from the side of the frame his view was limited by the deep embrasure. He could see only a table. But on the table, beside a candle flaring in its candlestick, lay three muskets. He moved so that he could see more fully into the room, and the reason for the screaming was instantly clear.

A girl with long fair hair, clad in a nightdress, was standing with both arms stretched high above her head. She stood thus because the rope that bound her wrists was passed over an oak beam that spanned the walls and hauled tight. The nightdress had been ripped open and revealed her breasts. A man in a black uniform jacket – Mr Fitton could only see his back – was standing in front of her with what looked like a carving-knife in his hand. He shouted at the girl and the words came clearly.

'*L'eau de vie! Où est-il – hein?*'

On the last word he pricked the flesh between her breasts with the point of his knife, drawing a bead of blood, and she uttered a piercing scream.

Mr Fitton's purview showed him only part of the room but he didn't doubt that there were other people in it, including two more Black Legionaries on the hunt for hidden brandy. The boast that one Englishman could thrash three Frenchmen had never impressed him, and he was unarmed, but action he must take, and at once. This was no time to consider plans and weigh consequences. He ran to the nearest stone wall, wrenched a sizeable rock from its top, and dashed back to hurl it with all his force through the window.

The crash and clatter of his missile were followed by a babel of startled shouts and oaths, which he heard indistinctly, for he was darting round to the front of the house. Five seconds after launching the rock he was flattening himself against the outer side of one of the big flakes forming the porch.

Almost at once the door was flung open and two men came rushing out and round to the side whence the rock had been thrown. They were carrying their muskets.

One man at least was left in the house, no doubt to watch over their victim. Mr Fitton craned his head round the porch and shouted hoarsely and urgently.

'*Hé, là! Venez! Venez vitement!*'

It worked like a charm. A third man came charging out and ran shouting to find his comrades. He, too, carried a musket. Mr Fitton, who had hoped he might leave it behind for his own use, was out of his hiding-place and into the house in a breathing space. The door leading to the candle-lit room was open; the lock of the outer door had been smashed. He dashed into the inner room, threw a quick glance round him, and swung the door shut; it had a bolt and socket that would hold against forced entry, if only for a few minutes. He shot the bolt and turned to survey the room.

There was the girl, half-suspended from the cross-beam and staring at him, her eyes wide with terror. There was a man in what looked like a flannel nightshirt lying motionless in a corner by the big empty fireplace. They were the only people in the room. An open flight of wooden steps led up to a floor above and below it a door indicated a further room.

'Don't be afraid,' he told the girl, and picked up the carving-knife from the table.

The rope, which was a thin one, had been secured to the leg of a heavy dresser that stood against the wall. He cut it and the girl sank to the floor, to get up again as soon as her wrists were freed and run to the man lying in the corner. Her agonized cry of '*Tad!*' wrung his heart and he went to kneel beside her.

'Your father?' he asked.

'They have killed him!' She clutched the blood-spotted nightgown to her breast and glanced fearfully at him. 'There iss no brandy here, sir – 'twas took to Trehowel.'

Mr Fitton was gently raising the man's grey head; the

movement produced a groan. In the same instant he heard outside the heavy footsteps of the men returning from their vain search.

'He's been stunned,' he said rapidly. 'Get water. Bathe this wound on his forehead. Give him some to drink.'

He sprang to his feet. It was time to look to his defences. His glance passed over the broken window – it was a route of escape but he couldn't leave these people to the mercies of the French. They could fire into the room from that window, but their arc of fire would be limited. Using all his strength, he ran the heavy table against the bolted door. The thud of its impact was echoed by a loud knocking and a voice cried '*Ouvrez!*' and followed it with an oath.

He took the carving-knife in his hand. The candle? If they broke in he would dash it out – a knife against three muskets would have more chance in the dark. A musket-butt crashed against the door, and again. Its panels were much less stout than those of the outer door, and it would not hold out for long. He stood with his back against the wall beside the door, carving-knife ready to strike if a hand reached through the splintered door. The next heavy blow drove one of the panels inward. He raised his knife.

But there came no other blow. Instead here was a startled exclamation, and he heard the tramp of many feet approaching. A voice shouted the order to halt and then came from nearer at hand.

'*Qu'est-ce qu' arrive ici? Sacrébleu! Rendez-vous, les trois – Dubois, prenez ces hommes-là!*'

A scuffle of feet and a clash of protesting voices followed and were cut short by what sounded like a series of blows. A moment later someone knocked on the splintered door and rattled the bolt. The same voice spoke again, this time on a cajoling note.

'You that's inside! Will you be opening this door, now? I swear by the Holy Patrick you'll come to no harm.'

Mr Fitton hauled the table back. He was in no case to stand a siege, and it seemed likely that this newcomer meant what he said. But he was taking no chances.

'You can come in,' he said, 'and you'll come very slowly.'

He drew the bolt and stood back. The door edged gently open and a tall young man stepped cautiously into the room. He wore the uniform of the Black Legion, with a good deal of gold braid on the cuffs and shoulders of his jacket. His slow glance round the candle-lit room took in the girl tending her father in the corner, the broken window, and Mr Fitton with his carving-knife. His face, beneath a triple-cocked hat set on black curls, would have been handsome but for the loose-lipped mouth that now widened in a grin.

'Is it St George you are, and I the dragon?' he said. 'Be easy now, Mr What's-the-name, and tell me what's been happening here.'

Mr Fitton put his knife on the table. 'Three of your men were torturing the girl to make her tell where the brandy was hidden,' he said succinctly.

'Bedad, they're no men of mine! They're Tate's jail-birds and they're under arrest this minute, the scoundrels. I've twenty regulars of the Sambre regiment with me and the general's orders to —' He stopped and suddenly frowned. 'But you're no Welshman, and that's a uniform jacket, a Navy jacket by the look of it. How come you here?'

'I chanced to be passing and heard the girl scream.'

'Ah, come now!' The young man wagged his head reprovingly. 'I'll be wanting more than that from you. Consider, my dear man — an English sea-officer flourishing carving-knives in a Welsh farmhouse don't make sense. Sure, 'twould make a pig curious. For a start, I'll have your name and the name of your ship.'

His breath, Mr Fitton was able to notice, smelled of brandy and his blue eyes were slightly bloodshot.

'Fitton, master's mate in HMS *Curlew*,' he said.

'The devil you are. Well, Mr Fitton, it's the prisoner of Barry St Leger you are – lieutenant in the Black Legion and at your service. Where's your ship?'

It was Mr Fitton's turn to wag his head. 'Oh no, Mr St Leger. As a prisoner of war I've given all the information required of me.'

The lieutenant sat himself negligently on the table and regarded him with mock sadness.

'I'd half-settled you were a gentleman like meself,' he said, 'and now you're talking like a lawyer. I'll have to remind you I'm an officer of the Black Legion. We have ways of making prisoners talk.'

'I don't doubt it.' Mr Fitton was nettled. 'One of Colonel Tate's Red Indian tortures, perhaps. I recall his preference for what he called Redskin warfare.'

'What's this?' St Leger said, staring. 'You're acquainted with the general?'

'I have that honour,' said Mr Fitton drily. 'Though he was a mere colonel when he told me of his plans a month ago.'

'Told you of his – by the Holy Patrick, this beats all!' St Leger slid off the table and stood glaring uncertainly at his prisoner. 'What the devil are you, man? A French agent?'

Mr Fitton's mention of the colonel had been purely fortuitous, but he perceived that he might turn it to temporary advantage.

'Mr St Leger,' he said portentously, 'my situation is one of some delicacy.' That at least was true. 'To explain it to you would involve a breach of secrecy. Your general, however, is aware of my avocation and will vouch for it. Moreover, I have certain information to lay before him. Your best plan, if I may suggest it, is to bring me to General Tate.'

The Irishman pulled off his hat with a despairing gesture and scratched his head, eyeing Mr Fitton doubtfully the while.

'Damn me if I know whether to believe you,' he said at last. 'Devil a word I've heard of any agent, or information, or suchlike flummery.'

'You've heard of Madame de Callac, I dare say,' Mr Fitton said at a venture.

St Leger's eyes opened wide. 'So that's it!' he exclaimed. 'You're her man – and the dead spit of a bloody Englishman, too. Why the deuce couldn't you say so at first? And what are you doing here?'

'I answer no questions except to General Tate.'

Mr Fitton's tone was now peremptory. He had swiftly resolved to adopt the part thus thrust upon him, not because he had any hope of maintaining it for long – Tate would put an end to his pretence as soon as he saw him – but because he was not going to miss a chance of seeing the enigmatic colonel again. After a moment's hesitation St Leger shrugged his shoulders and nodded.

'So be it,' he said abruptly. 'I'll bring you to the general, Mr Fitton, and you'll be marching two miles with my detachment.'

He glanced round. At the other end of the room, the grey-haired man was sitting with his back against the wall while his daughter bathed his head. He went to them and swept off his hat.

'It's sorry I am you've had this trouble,' he said, his eyes on the girl's torn nightgown, 'and if it wasn't that I'm on duty I'd stay to comfort you, my dear.'

With that, he clapped his hat on again and returned to Mr Fitton.

'Now, sir – or should it be monsieur? – we'll march to Trehowel. 'Tis where we've established headquarters. You'd be marching there as a prisoner if you hadn't tipped me the wink,' he added, pulling the shattered door open. 'After you, if you please.'

As the door closed behind them on the candle-lit room Mr Fitton reflected that in less than an hour he would be a prisoner indeed; if, that was, he was allowed to remain alive. His hasty dissimulation made him a spy. And spies, as he had heard, were shot.

3

The half-moon low in the west gave little light now and the yard outside the house was dark. It was crowded with the black figures of men and astir with the shuffle of feet and low-voiced talk. St Leger's sharp command brought comparative silence, and he conferred for a few moments with one who was apparently a sergeant. Mr Fitton's recent reflections had impelled him to look for a possible way of escape as soon as he emerged from the porch, but his sight was impaired by the sudden change from light to darkness, and he could only guess at the whereabouts of the gate leading to the open slopes above the cliffs. In any case, he told himself, to make a dash for freedom would be the merest folly, with twenty muskets threatening his back. And even if he escaped being shot while climbing or opening the gate, he would lead the inevitable pursuit to *Curlew*.

St Leger, he perceived, had a bottle or flask tilted to his lips. The lieutenant turned and held it out to him.

'Take a drain by the way of a stirrup-cup,' he said genially. 'Sure, there's no stirrups, but shanks's mare will go the easier for a sup of right cognac.'

Mr Fitton thanked him and took a sip from the big leathern flask, which was nearly empty. It was excellent brandy, and he said so as he handed it back.

'Why wouldn't it be? There's a dozen ankers of it, contraband, in the cellar at Trehowel, under guard night and day.' St Leger corked the flask and handed it to the sergeant. 'Dubois carries my provender for me. He's the only sergeant in the armies of the Republic that doesn't like brandy.' He began to laugh but checked himself. 'We'd best be moving. – *Formez!*'

At his shout the dark figures shuffled themselves into some sort of order. Mr Fitton, whose night-sight was fast improving, could make out that the three prisoners, his late opponents, had been secured in single file, each roped to the next by a loop knotted round his neck and the bight of the rope held by a man behind them. The soldiers of the Sambre regiment stood in double file, half of them in front of the prisoners and half behind. St Leger gave the order to march and the little column passed out of the yard, the lieutenant and Mr Fitton bringing up the rear.

The cart-track underfoot climbed steeply round a corner of hillside, and Mr Fitton had to force himself on the uphill trudge. He was physically and mentally tired. The past eight hours had been exacting; his legs were weary and his feet, in shoes now nearing disintegration, were very sore. He comforted himself with the reflection that but for a lucky chance he would have made a fourth in the neck-roped file ahead.

It was soon evident that St Leger's draught of brandy had been a deep one. His stride was more than a little unsteady, and from time to time he lurched sideways to brush against Mr Fitton's shoulder. He seemed to have accepted his companion as the French agent he himself had named him and gave free rein to his brandy-loosened tongue.

'If these three murdering spalpeens found no brandy yonder,' he said, 'it must be the only farm for miles around that hasn't got gallons of the stuff stored away. A wrecked cargo, I'm after hearing. And that's our trouble at this minute, as you'll see.'

'Your men found this liquor?' Mr Fitton prompted as the lieutenant paused on a prolonged hiccup.

'Damn them to blazes! 'Twas the jail-birds went foraging without orders. Wasn't I warning Le Brun – that's our second-in-command – to keep a tight hand on them? *Banditti*, that's what they are.'

The track, which had made a slight descent, steepened in another rise and St Leger saved his breath while they breasted it. From far in front came the crack of a musket-shot.

'Hark to 'em!' the lieutenant panted wrathfully. 'Every man-jack has a musket and ammunition. 'Tis wasting powder in *feux-de-joie* they are, and drunk as pigs with it. If there's not two hundred and more spread hither and yon across this bloody wilderness I'm an Orangeman – lying under bushes drinking themselves stupid. And as many more raising tallywhack round the fires, bad cess to them! I've served in armies, Mr Mitton – Fitton – but I've never seen a shambles like this.'

He paused for breath. Mr Fitton remained silent; information was coming to him without his questioning. The track was bringing them round the hillside, heading east so far as he could judge, with dark slopes falling away on the left. There was no more light from the vanished moon and the stars were hidden, and they marched in that deeper darkness that precedes the dawn. There was light, however, in front, the glow of ruddy light above the French encampment, and through the crunch of marching feet on the rough surface he could hear a continuous murmur of sound which grew as they advanced.

And St Leger continued to talk; as much, it seemed, to relieve his feelings as to converse with the man beside him. His voice was thick and he stammered now and then. He and the two other Irish officers, Tyrrell and Morrison, had been sent out (Mr Fitton gathered) with patrols to seek and bring back the wandering marauders – a hopeless quest at dead of night in a strange and tangled countryside. The three prisoners were all they were likely to find until a wider search by daylight could be made. That search would take many hours, and if and when all the delinquents had been brought in, most of them would be helpless from the effects of drink. If the general had any idea of moving his army before the next nightfall he'd better abandon it. The whole business made Tipperary Fair look like a model of order beside it. Two of his friends in the Irish regiment, St Leger said bitterly, had prophesied just such a pigsty muddle and had stayed in France.

'And it's sorry I am I didn't stay with them!' he added, rendered oblivious by brandy to caution. 'Wasn't it to fight the English we joined this bloody Legion – meself and Morrison and Tyrrell? Bristol, 'twas said we'd march on, and here we are landed in Wales. We've no quarrel with the Welsh. Oh, says the general, the Welsh will join with us, they misliking the English. Sorra a Welshman will join after all this rick-burning and plundering and torturing of girls!'

Apparently perceiving, belatedly, that the rear men of his column could hear what he was saying, he checked himself and began again on a less discouraging note.

'Mind you, Mr Fitton, the issue's not in doubt. It's known they can't bring any force to oppose us – a quarter of our numbers is the best they'll do. By tomorrow we'll have every man on his feet and by the Holy Patrick Fishguard's ours. *Vive la République!*'

The histrionic fervour with which he uttered this last sentiment was somewhat spoiled by the loud hiccup that followed it. A moment later he stumbled heavily over a break in the uneven track and would have fallen heavily but that Mr Fitton grasped his arm. St Leger grunted his thanks and thereafter lapsed into silence, no doubt devoting all his attention to keeping on his feet.

The track was running level now along the brow of the hill, and the widespread fires of the encampment lay scarcely half a mile away below on their left front. The murmur of sound had swelled to a distant uproar, a mingling of shouts and wild yells and raucous singing.

Pencaer by Moonlight

Mr Fitton, whose experience of dealing with drunken British seamen was considerable, didn't envy those whose task it was to bring order to several hundred drunken French criminals. To restore them to the likeness of disciplined troops would surely take more than twenty-four hours; and, as St Leger had said, the countryside would have to be scoured for the uncounted marauders who had strayed farther afield. It seemed certain that the day now approaching its dawn would see no attack on Fishguard. If that was so it was good news – as far as it went; but it would take Knox and his fellow-officers more than twenty-four hours to raise a force sufficient to repel the attack.

He thought of *Curlew*. If she could be got round to Fishguard she might assist in its defence. Even if her guns couldn't range on the French encampment, she could provide another thirty or forty fighting men –

A shout and a scuffle at the front of the column interrupted his reflections. The men in front of him came to a sudden halt and St Leger ran stumbling forward. There was a crackling of twigs in the thickets down on the left of the track, and then St Leger came back, shouting the order to march on as he came.

'Two men crossed the road in front of us,' he said. 'Dubois wanted to fire on them but I wouldn't have it – you can't tell a Frenchman from a Welshman when it's as black as Barney's hat. Still and all, there's but ten minutes more and we'll be at Trehowel.'

Before they had gone three hundred paces the column halted again, this time at the challenge of a sentry. St Leger shouted his name and they marched on again, now between hedgerows and with trees above and below the track. Lights winked yellow between the trunks of larger trees grouped at a lower level, and they turned left to a gate guarded by another sentry. Barns and outbuildings loomed close in front and beyond them a large farmhouse whose every window shone with light.

Trehowel was a much larger house than Caerlem. John Mortimer's farm, Sam Evans had said it was, and John Mortimer was evidently a man of substance; Mr Fitton hoped he had got safely away before his dwelling had been seized and occupied as the Black Legion's headquarters. They passed a long low barn between lane and house from which came an indescribable medley of groans and shouts and gabbled talk. A man with a musket stood guard over its door.

'Those are the runagates we've brought in so far,' St Leger said. 'Two dozen at most. Half of 'em blind to the world and the rest – well, you can hear the creatures.'

He shouted the order to halt and the party shuffled to a standstill on the stones of the courtyard that ran along one side of the house. Light streamed from an open door, glinting on the musket of the black-uniformed sentry who stood beside it. St Leger gave rapid instructions to Dubois and turned to grasp Mr Fitton's arm.

'And now, my close-mouthed friend,' he said, 'you can loose your tongue to General Tate.'

7   The Hostage

1

The sentry at the door of Trehowel brought his musket to his side with a click as Lieutenant St Leger, followed by Mr Fitton, passed into a candle-lit passage. Three men in officers' uniforms were standing there talking in low-voiced French, and one of them turned as St Leger came in.

'Is it yourself, Barry?' he said. 'What fortune did ye have?'

'Three, and walking sober,' St Leger returned.

'Then ye did better than Morrison,' said the other with a chuckle. 'He found seven, but they were running drunk and gave him the slip.'

'What's more, I've one of Madame's men with me – says he has information for the general.' St Leger drew Mr Fitton past the three. 'He'd best see him now.'

'Morrison's in with him this minute.'

'This can't wait.'

St Leger pushed open a door and paused for a moment on the threshold. Mr Fitton, peering over his shoulder, found himself looking at the leader and originator of the Black Legion.

The room, lit by half a dozen candles, was the big farmhouse kitchen and a log fire blazed in the cavernous fireplace. A long table occupied the centre of the room and a man was seated at it, facing the door, addressing a stocky red-haired officer who stood at the table's side. The seated man was not the Quaker-looking Colonel Tate that he remembered. The general's long white hair was gathered into a neat queue and tied with black ribbon. He wore a dashing uniform coat of bright blue with scarlet facings, open to show a white waistcoat with glittering gold buttons, and the cocked hat lying on the table beside him was decorated with a tricolor cockade. The long deep-furrowed face with its beaky nose looked older than Mr Fitton remembered it; but the slow, slightly nasal voice now raised in anger was not the voice of an old man.

'– and I expect my orders to be obeyed without question!' the general was saying ponderously. 'Without question, Captain Morrison!'

'Och, I'll obey orders, *mon Général*,' Morrison said sullenly. 'But I'm telling you it's waste of time to seek out these fellows in the dark. If you'd take my advice and wait –'

'What the Eternal have I to do with your advice? Take your men and do as I've ordered!'

Tate's voice had risen suddenly to a note of almost hysterical anger that brought a stare of surprise from Morrison. Then the captain saluted stiffly, turned on his heel, and came towards the door.

'Bloody old fool!' he muttered below his breath as he pushed past the two in the doorway.

'Lieutenant St Leger!' The general's voice had lost its hint of hysteria. 'You can advance and make your report.'

St Leger beckoned Mr Fitton to follow and stepped to the table.

'As ordered, sir, I searched the area south-west of the camp. I found three men and brought them back under guard. I also found this gentleman.' He plucked his companion's sleeve and drew him forward. ' 'Tis an acquaintance of yours, according to himself.'

Tate's eyes had widened as they fell on Mr Fitton's face, and he sat forward in his chair.

'Well, I do declare!' he said slowly.

'He calls himself Fitton,' St Leger continued, swaying slightly on his feet and supporting himself with a hand on Mr Fitton's shoulder. 'Playing at St George he was, defending a farmhouse against three poxy dragons of soldiers wishful to find brandy. And why wouldn't he, with a fair young maiden *en négligée* waiting to —'

'That will do!' snapped the general. 'Why was he in this farmhouse?'

'Devil a word would he say to my questioning, sir, but that he'd information to lay before you, and that you knew him.'

The general's gaze had not shifted itself from Mr Fitton's expressionless face. His wide mouth puckered in a smile.

'Why, certainly I know Mr Michael Fitton,' he drawled. 'How do you get along, Mr Fitton?'

'Rather better, I fancy, than you do yourself, colonel,' Mr Fitton responded coolly. 'Your army seems to have got somewhat out of hand, if I may say so.'

Tate frowned annoyance; but not, it appeared, at this piece of impudence.

'You are ignorant, I opinionate, of my promotion,' he said stiffly. 'I hold the rank of *chef de brigade*, my friend. I am to be addressed as general.'

'I beg your pardon, general.'

The general turned to St Leger. 'Mr Fitton is an officer in the British Navy. We have met —'

'But that's a disguise, sir,' the lieutenant broke in. 'He's Madame's man, as he told me — Madame de Callac.'

'I told you nothing of the sort, Mr St Leger,' Mr Fitton said quickly. 'You told me that. It was not for me to contradict you.'

'And Mr Fitton is most certainly a naval officer,' Tate

drawled. 'I guess the credit of taking our first British prisoner is yours, lieutenant.'

'Well, that beats all!' St Leger exclaimed. 'But still and all – 'twas he named Madame to me.'

'He presumed, lieutenant, on a slight acquaintance with that charming lady, of which she has informed me.' Tate's pale eyes flickered curiously at his prisoner. ''pears to me, Mr Fitton, that the Almighty has ordained that your path and mine shall cross at more points than one.'

A similar idea had occurred to Mr Fitton, though he would have attributed it differently.

'And now, my friend,' the general continued, 'you will please to tell me what brings you on shore here. Your claim to have information for me was a subterfuge, I conclude.'

'Not at all, general,' Mr Fitton rejoined equably. 'I have information which you should hear and – if you're a man of sense – act upon instantly.'

He had considered his course and decided on it. There was only the slightest of chances that it would save Fishguard but it must be tried.

'I'm ashore to bring news of your landing to the military authorities here. That was done –' he took out his watch and consulted it – 'four hours ago. By now the militia and the yeomanry, the garrisons from Pembroke and Cardigan, are on the march. They'll have three times your numbers and field artillery as well. You've just the one hope of escaping defeat and imprisonment. Get yourself and your Black Legion into those four ships, General Tate, and back with you to France.'

There was a moment's pause and then St Leger burst out laughing.

'H-Holy P-Patrick!' he cried, choking on his laughter. 'But that was bravely crowed!'

The general chuckled and wagged his head in mock solemnity.

'I'm most uncommon grateful for your warning, my friend,' he said gravely, 'and darned if I wouldn't take your advice — but for two things. The first is that I haven't four ships to embark in, for they have already sailed. The second is that the information I've gotten is more accurate than yours. I know beyond a peradventure that if the British can bring three hundred men to face me within three days that's the most they can do, and they'll need to be cruel smart to do that. As for artillery, the Black Legion will be a week's march away before a gun can be dragged to Fishguard.'

It was the reply Mr Fitton had expected and he knew it to be not far from the truth. None the less Tate's contemptuous tone annoyed him.

'Your army's a rabble and you know nothing of the country,' he said shortly. 'You've no —'

'That's a lie!' Tate shouted, suddenly enraged. 'My Black Legion can whip anything King George can send against me, by the Eternal! There's not a man among your squires and farmers that has my experience of warfare! See here!'

He stood up, kicking back his chair, and stalked to the wall, where a large sheet of paper had been tacked to the panelling. It bore a crude map or diagram done in red and black inks.

'Fishguard!' He stabbed a shaking finger at the map. 'Trehowel, where my main force is encamped. Between them the bay, which they call Goodwick Sands — oh yes, Mr Fitton, Samuel Evans gave me the names. I've four hundred men already deployed on this hill Carnwnda, overlooking the bay, and two hundred more where this valley debouches on the sands. Those sands, Mr Fitton, dry out for the better part of a mile at low tide and low tide's at ten tomorrow. By then I'll have fourteen hundred men in order for attack. I shall march them down to those sands and straight across to take Fishguard.'

'And sorra a hope will there be for Fishguard,' St Leger muttered.

Tate ignored the interruption; but it seemed to recall him to a less excited state of mind.

'If there's resistance I shall crush it without mercy,' he went on in a calmer tone. 'From Fishguard I shall take a guide for my onward march, and I'll have hostages to ensure he don't lead me astray. I've burned my boats, Mr Fitton, like other conquerors before me, and I calculate I'll bring fire and sword to Chester inside a week.' He showed his teeth in an unpleasant grin. 'And on my way there, my friend, I'll cut a mighty wide swathe – of a red colour.'

'Why?'

Mr Fitton's sharp question seemed to disconcert the general for a moment. His pale eyes flickered strangely as he stared at his prisoner.

'Why?' he repeated harshly.

'Yes – why?' Mr Fitton, stirred from his habitual calm, spoke fiercely. 'You'll slaughter innocent men and women who have no part in the war. How in God's name will this aid the cause of France?'

'And what the Eternal do I care for the cause –'

Tate pulled himself up short, with a side-glance at the attentive St Leger. He turned and sat down in his chair, set his hands on the table, and leaned slowly forward. He looked like an ageing wolf about to spring.

'I'll tell you why, Mr Michael Fitton,' he said in a voice that was half a snarl. 'Because twenty years ago the British employed Mohawk Indians in their army of America. Because those Mohawk Indians killed my parents – murdered my father and mother, Mr Fitton – scalped them, if you know what that means. Because I've waited twenty years for this chance and by heaven I'll not waste it! I'll have blood for blood!' the snarl had become a screech. 'British blood – rivers of blood! They shall pay – strike and spare not is the order – no prisoners – blood for blood!' His voice cracked on the word and he brandished a claw-like hand aloft. 'What d'ye know about that, Mr Michael Fitton?'

'I know this, William Tate,' Mr Fitton said quietly. 'You are mad.'

For an instant he thought Tate was going to attack him; the general had sprung to his feet, shaking and spluttering with fury. The foam on his lips glistened in the candle-light. Then he collapsed into his chair again, covered his eyes with one hand, and gestured urgently at St Leger with the other.

'Take him away!' he said shakily. 'Get rid of him.'

'What – string him up?' St Leger said doubtfully.

'No – no!'

'You said no prisoners, sir –'

'I may need a hostage. Hold him safe.'

The lieutenant beckoned to Mr Fitton. 'Come on with you, then. – The far barn, sir, with a man to guard him?'

The reply was a mumble. 'Where you will, but hold him safe.'

'Yes, sir.' St Leger touched his hat. 'Fitton, in front of me. To the door – march.'

Mr Fitton marched. At the door he shot a quick glance backward. General Tate was sitting with his white head on his hands. He looked an old, shrunken man.

There was no one in the dimly-lit passage. St Leger tapped his charge on the shoulder and bade him halt.

'Will it be a pistol you have in your pocket?' he demanded sharply.

'A telescopic glass.' Mr Fitton produced it. 'I've also a watch, a scrap of meat, and a crust of bread. If it's plunder you're after –'

'I'm not a robber, curse you! Get on!'

If he had any thought of making a dash for it when they reached the open air, Mr Fitton abandoned it. The yard was busy with men, parties of Black Legionaries departing and arriving, sergeants and officers bawling orders. He was surprised to find that it was no longer dark. The pale twilight of dawn was here, to reveal the details of the black uniforms and the unshaven features of the men. At St Leger's yell two men came trotting up, musket in hand. He gave them curt orders in rapid French, and Mr Fitton was marched away with a soldier on either hand and St Leger following, up the slope of the entrance lane to a stone building set back among the roadside thickets. A heavy wooden door grated open and he was thrust inside.

'I'm placing a sentry by this door and his musket's loaded,' the lieutenant told him. 'Sweet dreams, Mister Hostage – I wish I had the chance of 'em!'

The door banged shut and a heavy bar fell into place. The footsteps of two men receded outside. The sentry cleared his throat and spat. Mr Fitton stood in a darkness smelling of musty straw.

He swayed as he stood. He had been exerting himself, on foot or on horseback, for eight hours without rest and he was conscious now of utter weariness. He shuffled across the uneven floor until his feet found a heap of straw, and sank down on the straw with a groan of relief. Hunger and thirst were less urgent than his desire for sleep; but habit was stronger. Almost without being aware of it, he took his watch from his fob and began to wind it.

2

The watch was still in his hand when he woke. There was light flooding into his prison from a little cobwebbed window high in the stone wall and the dial was plain: two minutes after noon. He had slept for nearly eight hours.

The sound of departing footsteps suggested that it had been the changing of his sentry that had awakened

The Hostage   161

him. Beyond that sound other noises came muffled to his ears – marching feet, shouted orders, the faint shrilling of a distant bugle-call. General Tate, he remembered, must be routing out the last of his straying revellers, doing his utmost to rebuild some hundreds of drink-sodden rogues into military shape again, to restore his Black Legion to its full fighting strength of 1,400 men. Was it possible that he would succeed in time to launch his attack today?

He got up somewhat stiffly from his couch in the straw and looked about him. He was in a stone barn with a beamed and slated roof. The dung on the stone-slabbed floor and the long mangers on the walls told that it had housed kine not long ago, but it was empty now except for some leathern halters slung on a hook and the straw, piled against the inner wall, which had given him so long and reviving a sleep. But there had been additions to its furnishings while he slept. On the slabs near the door stood a bucket, a pitcher of water, and half-a-loaf wrapped in a torn cloth; someone (perhaps Lieutenant St Leger) had notions above the starvation of prisoners. As he bent to inspect these not unwelcome provisions he could see, through a crack in the door, the movement of a black uniform a yard or two away. The door had no fastening on its inner side; the bar he had heard drop into its socket, and the sentry's musket, were sufficient to forbid any escape by that route.

He sat down again on the straw to satisfy thirst and hunger, thriftily eating first the bread and meat from his pocket. The half-loaf was stale but good bread, the spoil no doubt of Trehowel pantry. He ate two-thirds of it, pocketing the rest against future need, and then set himself to consider his position.

What Tate could want with a hostage was a mystery. Mr Fitton had no illusions as to his own importance in such a role; a threat to hang or dismember him would scarcely have weight enough to halt such meagre forces as might oppose the Black Legion. Perhaps the general, faced with the alternatives of having him shot or holding him prisoner, had been unable to bring himself to do murder. That self-avowed craving for the blood of all Britishers, however, might make him change his mind. And what would he do with his prisoner when the Black Legion, having got itself into marching order, began its advance on Fishguard? It was clear that if there was any chance of getting out of this barn unscathed he had better seek it. He finished the water from the pitcher and got to his feet.

The window high in the wall was his first consideration. Its stone sill was within reach of his upstretched hands, and if he smashed the dirty glass he might squeeze through it. That meant noise which would alert the sentry, and he would have to emerge head first above a six-foot drop, which would very probably land him upside down in the sentry's clutches. There was little prospect of success here. He turned his attention to the inner wall. This, as he had already observed, was a partition wall dividing the barn into two halves, of which his prison was one. It was solidly built of hewn stone and filled all the ten-foot height of the barn. He pulled the straw away from its base but there was no weakness there; the cement between the oblong stones was fresh and to prise out one of the blocks would take days even if he had a tool to work with, which he hadn't. Moreover, the chamber on the other side would almost certainly have a door barred as securely as the door at this end. All things considered, the idea of escaping from the barn might be dismissed.

Mr Fitton had always considered that the Fox, in the fable of the Fox and the Grapes, was more deserving of praise than of contempt. Surely it was more philosophical, more productive of a contented mind, to decide that grapes out of reach were probably sour grapes anyway,

The Hostage

than to give way to frustration and disappointment. So he sat down again on the straw and reflected that if he did succeed in breaking out of the barn and dodging the sentry's shot, he would still have to win clear of an area swarming with Black Legionaries. *True instruction is this: learning to will that things should happen as they do.* Old Epictetus set a hard task but there was nothing for it but to try and follow his precept.

All the same, the afternoon hours passed very slowly. There was plenty to listen to from the invisible outside and he employed himself in trying to deduce what was happening. Bugle-calls sounded at irregular intervals from far and near, interspersed with peremptory shouting; it might be that some sort of drill or rehearsal for attack was taking place. Twice large troops of men passed along the lane above the barn, one of them at the double. Once there was a prolonged screeching as of a man in pain, and he envisaged one of the refractory jail-birds receiving a merited punishment with the lash. It was within a minute of four o'clock by his watch when he heard the guard being changed outside his prison-barn; whatever the disorder of Tate's army there was plainly order and punctuality in the neighbourhood of its headquarters. The newcomer exchanged a few gruff words with the departing sentry, but though Mr Fitton had his ear to the crack of the door he could only make out one phrase – *je m'en fiche*.

He could be sure, now, that no attack would take place today. One detail of the general's crude map had impressed itself on his memory – the narrowness of the land approach to Fishguard. At the head of the bay that lay between the town and the Black Legion's position was a wide marshy valley. The only approach road ran between marsh and bay, crossing the outlet stream by a bridge – it had been plainly marked on the map. Unless Tate waited until low water, when he could deploy his army and advance across the sands according to his declared intention, he would have to approach Fishguard by that narrow road with his men in column, the rear of his force some half-mile behind the van. And by now the sands – Goodwick Sands, Tate had called them – were impassable under the tide. He might be mad; but he was not mad enough to attack by that road.

The small window admitted only a little light and that light was already beginning to fade. Mr Fitton, remembering that in an hour it would be sunset of a February day, set himself to put his house in order. He piled the straw into a more comfortable bed, and then sat down on it to examine his feet. About his broken shoes he could do nothing, but the blisters and raw-rubbed places he contrived to ease with paddings made from the cloth that had wrapped the loaf. He had finished this, and was taking experimental paces to test the padding, when he heard steps approaching and the shuffle and click of the sentry coming to attention. The door was opened and St Leger came in, followed by a soldier carrying a pitcher of water and a small sack. The lieutenant glanced briefly at the prisoner before telling the man to empty the bucket and bring it back. The door, left open as the man obeyed, attracted Mr Fitton's eye and St Leger noticed it.

' 'Twould do you no good to make a dash for it,' he said with a grin. 'What's more, I've a pistol in my pocket and I'd use it, though it's sorry I'd be to shoot you.'

He looked tired, and there was a wild glitter in his eye that suggested brandy.

'I won't trouble you to take your pistol out, Mr St Leger,' Mr Fitton assured him drily.

The soldier came back with the empty bucket and St Leger snapped an order at him as he went out again.

'I've dined meself,' he said, 'as a man as discerning as Mr Michael Fitton will have noted. Oh, I know your sort of Englishman – takes all in and gives nothing out. How I hate the breed!' He checked himself on a hiccup. 'No offence, no offence. I'm after saying I've dined meself and I've brought your own dinner.'

He waved an unsteady hand at the sack and the pitcher which his man had deposited in a corner. Mr Fitton thanked him and he twirled the hand in a deprecatory gesture.

'Ah, 'twas the general's order. Either he's taken a liking for you or he's fattening you for the slaughter. But the half-bottle of Margaux was my idea. What is life to the man without wine? – And that's Ecclesiasticus for you.'

Mr Fitton thanked him again. 'The general, I trust, has recovered from his indisposition of this morning?' he inquired.

St Leger laughed. 'Indisposition, is it? He's worse, Fitton – head in the clouds and dreaming he's a second Marlborough. You'd think our fourteen hundred was fourteen thousand. "My army", he says to us, "my army will take up battle position at first light tomorrow", he says, looking like the King of Tara addressing his chieftains. And what would be facing us but a little small town with not a professional soldier in it.'

'You attack tomorrow, then?'

St Leger, who had settled himself with his shoulders against the wall, paused before replying.

'Sure, there's no harm in telling you. We've collected and drubbed sober all but a dozen men and we attack at ten tomorrow, if attack is what you'd be calling it. There's not a fifth of our numbers to oppose us, and they no more than untrained yokels wearing uniforms.'

'Can you be sure of that?'

'Why wouldn't I be? Haven't we had observation on the town all day from Carnwnda hill? 'Tis less than two miles, and if Tyrrell's not lying he's counted fewer than two hundred militia. Blue coats and white breeches they wear, and they're deployed along the slopes below the town.' St Leger's sudden grimace was just visible in the dim light. 'By the Holy Patrick, I hope they'll take to their heels before they're slaughtered! Tate's order's out to give no quarter.'

'Mr St Leger,' said Mr Fitton suddenly, 'you heard me tell William Tate that I thought him mad. What's your own opinion?'

It was a moment before the lieutenant replied, and when he did so it was in a lowered voice and after a glance at the door beyond which stood the sentry.

'I'll own to you I've had my doubts, Fitton. He's a queer customer and that's putting it mildly. If we hadn't Lebrun as second-in-command — Lebrun's got his head well screwed on — I'm thinking the Black Legion would find itself —' He stopped. 'But this is fool's talk. We've landed and we march tomorrow.'

'What made you join this Black Legion?' Mr Fitton asked curiously.

'Why, for the fun of it, me boy!' St Leger's sudden gaiety sounded forced. 'No man of my name would turn aside from a venture like this — besides, 'tis a swipe at King George, which is what I enlisted for. March and fight,' he went on recklessly, 'bayonet the bloody redcoats — though devil a redcoat we'll see tomorrow — strike for Erin and down with tyranny! I'm in it and with it, Fitton, and I'll see it through. *Vogue la galère!*'

The thin high notes of a distant bugle-call echoed mockingly his defiant crow and he let out an oath.

'That's lights out. Curse the brandy — makes a man talk till all's blue. I'll have to grope a way to my pallet now.' He imitated the general's nasal tones. ' "Every man and every officer will get what sleep they can before dawn". That includes Barry St Leger, Mr Fitton, so I'll take my leave. I doubt we'll meet again.'

He turned to the door. Mr Fitton belatedly remembered his own dubious position.

'What's the general going to do with me?' he demanded quickly.

'God and the Virgin know – I don't. At a guess, I'd say he'll chain you to his chariot-wheels as a symbol of his triumph. Good night to you!'

The door closed behind St Leger, the heavy bar thudded into place. Mr Fitton heard the lieutenant stumble and curse as he hurried away, waited until the presence of a sentry was confirmed by the sound of a man whistling through his teeth, and then investigated his dinner. The pitcher contained water; in the sack were a small loaf, a leg of chicken, and a bottle half-full of wine. He carried these provisions to the pile of straw and sat down in the darkness to dine.

His stoicism gave him an invaluable capacity for living in the moment when occasion served; at this moment it was totally beyond his power to do anything about his own fate and that of Fishguard, so he enjoyed his meal with no thought but for the tenderness of the chicken and the excellence of the claret. He finished both, and then used some of the water from the pitcher to wash his hands and face. After that, he lay back on the straw and allowed his thoughts their freedom.

The multitudinous noises of the encampment had sunk to an indeterminate murmur like the distant rumour of the sea. What of *Curlew*, whose commander would be wondering what had become of him? Certainly Barrington wouldn't keep her in the Carregonnen bay on the chance that he would rejoin her there. By now, if her temporary repair had been successful, she would have come round into Fishguard harbour. Barrington would no doubt make his way to the defence headquarters – the Royal Oak tavern, he remembered – and place his seamen at the disposal of the militia commander. Sam Evans would be with them.

Despite his long sleep of last night he found himself getting drowsy. Perhaps the half-bottle of wine had something to do with that. The wine, he reflected idly, might have come over in the hold of Will Devonald's brig; Devonald, one of whose 'customers' was the lady of Long Warren.

Simone de Callac had entered his thoughts more than once in the past forty-eight hours, and he had thrust her out of them. Now he forced himself to face his problem; which was indeed no problem at all, for his course was obvious. She was a French spy, and if he ever got out of his present predicament he would have to report that to the authorities at the earliest possible opportunity. What would they do with her? Imprisonment in some filthy gaol was the least of the likely penalties. He recalled the lissom grace of her slight figure, the candid glance of her blue-grey eyes, the delicate air of aristocracy that she wore like a robe; and the vision of her in some dank prison-cell, perhaps with drunken slatterns and prostitutes for company, sickened him. To be the means of exposing her to months, perhaps years of ignominy was something he could not do. But then, he remembered suddenly, there was no need for him to do it – he was not the only man who knew Madame de Callac's real occupation. He had told Barrington, and Barrington would be sure to report it. That gave him relief, but only for a moment. Of course his own evidence would be required, and he was bound to give it. There could be no shirking on this issue.

Well, it was out of his power to save her. Besides, it was tantamount to treason even to wish to save an enemy of King George. With some difficulty he stifled his traitorous concern for Simone de Callac and sought refuge in philosophy. The matter was out of his power, therefore it was futile to worry about it. He was sleepy, and there was nothing whatever to do but sleep. After a while he slept.

3

He woke to find a pale daylight filtering through the cobwebs on the window, aware that he had been awakened by a sound and instantly realizing what the sound signified. The bugle brayed again from no great distance away – it was probably outside Trehowel farmhouse – and like some unnatural sequence of echoes other and more distant bugles answered it. This was the prelude to the attack on Fishguard.

Mr Fitton looked at his watch: six o'clock, and in an hour it would be sunrise. If General Tate had intended to move at first light he was late with his *réveille*; but then, he had no need to hurry. And the encampment was quickly astir. He could hear the medley of shouts as sergeants and corporals roused their men, and a rhythmic sound like faraway hoofbeats – the Black Legion had no horses so it must be a drum. He could also hear the heavy tread of feet from outside his door, a tread that neither approached nor receded. It was a cold morning and the sentry was stamping his feet to warm them.

Finding reliance on a single sense for information irksome, he went to peer through the crack of the door; but, though he could discern the movement of a black uniform a few yards away, the crack was too narrow to show him anything else except that there had been a white frost. He returned to his seat on the straw feeling unphilosophically resentful. His feet were a good deal more comfortable, and he was tired of his confinement. If he had been marched off with the Black Legion, whether to be shot or to be used in some unlikely way as a hostage, it would be better (he felt) than this enforced inaction.

A voice from the neighbourhood of Trehowel yelled

orders, and he heard a large body of men marching away along the lane. There was a hamlet called Llanwnda somewhere east along the hillside, he remembered, and in all probability the lane led to it; that detachment would no doubt move down to the slopes above Goodwick Sands where the rest of the Black Legion were forming. There would be paths nearer the coast by which other parties of Legionaries could march – but such speculations were useless when he had no real knowledge of the topography.

The vague sounds of footsteps and voices persisted for a while, became sparse, then ceased altogether. Even the sentry's stamping feet had stopped; the total silence was suggestive of a deserted encampment and the evacuation of Trehowel. Was he to be left here indefinitely, with the sentry to guard him? The answer to that came within ten minutes.

Boots clattered on the lane – a man running towards the barn. A breathless growl and a reply, both unintelligible. Then a thunderous knock on the door, followed by another and another – blows rather than knocks. He stood by the door and shouted.

'*Holà, dehors*! *Que faites-vous?*'

There was no reply to that, but a voice shouted '*Frappez*! *Frappez*!' and the blows redoubled. Suddenly they ceased and were replaced by rapidly-retreating footsteps. Eye and ear at the crack of the door assured him that both men had gone. They had driven a nail through the bar, pinning it to the doorpost, and left him unguarded. This was his chance.

Mr Fitton's desire for escape surprised himself by its intensity, but he went about its planning with characteristic coolness. The bar was ledged in a socket, so the nail could not be dislodged by any outward thrust he could compass. Upward leverage was the only method likely to succeed, and for that he needed a lever and a fulcrum. The only implements he possessed for this purpose were a chicken bone and a telescopic glass, both quite useless since the glass was far too thick to insert into the door-crack. The iron frame of the mangers should provide him with what he needed. He spent a long time wrenching and twisting at the rusted frames, while the daylight of a fine sunny morning grew and lit the barn, but whoever had fitted the mangers had done his work well and they were immovable. He rested for a while and then began to search the barn methodically, raking the straw aside and groping in the inner corners. There were dead leaves and a twig or two but nothing more. The leathern halters on the wall were no use, but the hook from which they depended might serve him. It took him twenty minutes of wrenching and wriggling to free the hook, which had been screwed into cement, and when he thrust it into the door-crack it would just touch the bar and no more. There was no escape for him by the door. There remained the window.

The sill of the window was well over six feet from the floor, and though he could get his fingertips over it the wall below it was too smooth to allow his toes any grip. After several attempts he had to admit defeat. With something to raise him farther from the floor he might get the flat of his hands on the sill and – perhaps – obtain sufficient leverage to hoist himself. His eye fell on the water-pitcher. He drank what was left of its contents before attempting to step up on it, and this was fortunate; it shattered into fragments as soon as his weight came on it.

It was not Mr Fitton's habit to swear, but he came near to it now. However the unphilosophical moment passed quickly, and after a brief consideration that assured him that escape was impossible, he sat down on the straw and consoled himself by breakfasting on the dry crust which was all he had left. He was munching the last of this when he heard the rapid tread of feet approaching on the lane. Two men, he judged, and in a hurry. They came to the door and shook its fastening. Mr Fitton stood up and took out his telescope, extending its full length. If that door was going to be opened, he was resolved to fight his way out of it.

'*Votre baionette, imbécile!*'

It was St Leger's voice. Sounds of furious straining and wrenching followed and after a moment the bar gave and the door flew open, revealing the lieutenant with a cocked pistol in his hand. Mr Fitton relaxed his tense pose, closed the telescope, and put it in his pocket.

'If I'm to breakfast on lead,' he said, 'you're late bringing it, Mr St Leger.'

St Leger disregarded this. 'Out with you!' he ordered harshly. 'You're wanted by the general.'

His face was dark with anger and wore an ugly scowl. Mr Fitton, stepping out through the doorway, saw that the second man was an undersized soldier with a bayonet affixed to his musket-barrel.

'*Marchez!*' St Leger barked at the man, and thrust the prisoner into place behind him.

With the lieutenant third in the short line, they moved off down the lane at a fast pace, past the entrance to Trehowel (deserted now) and up the short hill beyond.

'What's the general want with me?' Mr Fitton asked as they went.

The lieutenant made no reply except a disgusted grunt. They topped the hill, and the lane rounded a fold of the hillside to open a prospect of rocks and thickets sloping away on their left to the coast. Though the lane was in shadow the rough slope was sunlit, and the bar of sea beyond was misty blue. There was nothing to be seen of the Black Legion or of Fishguard Bay. Suddenly St Leger spoke from behind him, seemingly unable to contain his emotions.

'So you were right after all, curse you!'

The Hostage

Mr Fitton pricked up his ears. 'How so?'

'The bloody redcoats.' The words came in a snarl. 'They're in the town. A regiment of 'em and more coming in – you'll see the buggers plain from our front. God knows how it was managed but you'll likely pay for it yourself.'

'I don't see that I –'

'They're twice our numbers.' St Leger seemed to be talking to himself. 'They sent a flag of truce demanding our surrender – Holy Patrick, surrender!'

Mr Fitton's heart leapt. The miracle had happened!

'But Tate refused?' he said.

'He refused. But he'll make terms, God damn him to hell! Why would he send for you, else? You're a hostage – he'll use you in making his terms.'

'And suppose I decline to –'

'Ah, shut your mouth!' St Leger said savagely; and to the soldier in front, '*A gauche ici!*'

A narrow track diverged from the lane to plunge steeply down the hillside on their left. They had come farther round the corner of land and Mr Fitton could see a strip of Fishguard bay and its opposite shore, though the town was still hidden. On a knoll that rose from the tangle of thickets below them were two big heaps of unidentifiable articles with two or three men, small black figures, standing beside them; the Black Legion's equivalent of a baggage-train, he supposed. They started down the rough track, the soldier in the lead flicking aside over-arching brambles with his bayonet. The knoll sank from sight, walls of thorn bushes pressed close on either hand with grey mossy rocks crouching behind the bushes.

Mr Fitton, feigning to stumble on a projecting stone, managed to glance behind him. St Leger still had his pistol in his hand. He walked on, two paces behind the soldier, his eyes scanning the tall hedges of leafless thorns. The semblance of a gap appeared in the right-hand hedge twenty paces ahead and he braced himself. He dared not look round. His ear must locate the target.

'Mr St Leger,' he said impressively.

'Well?' The lieutenant's tone was peremptory.

'I shall owe you an apology.'

'For what?'

Mr Fitton was opposite the gap.

'For *this*!'

On the second word he spun round like a top on the ball of his left foot and his fist smashed into the side of the Irishman's head. St Leger went down like a log, his pistol exploding as he fell. The soldier halted and turned with a shout. But Mr Fitton was already into the gap and racing up a path that might have accommodated a goat but was a deal too constricted for a master's mate flying for his life.

8 Quixote at Fishguard

1

The path, a foot wide and contouring the slope of the hillside, dodged between head-high mounds of brambles whose trailing branches, hung with sheep's wool, caught at Mr Fitton's legs as he pelted along it. In fifty paces it dipped and rose again on a ridge of bare turf. Crossing this he was in view from the track below, and the flat report of a musket told that he had been seen. The bullet came nowhere near him and he ran on without slackening his pace, his one aim to put distance between himself and possible pursuit. He thought pursuit unlikely; his sore knuckles were proof that his blindly aimed blow had struck fair and square, rendering St Leger helpless for a minute or so at least. As for the soldier, it would take him two minutes to reload his musket, and by that time his target would be out of range.

The stony undulations of the path were trending continually to the right round the shoulder of the hill, threading a way through tall gorse bushes. Not far above him on that side was the lane they had left, the lane that (as he had speculated) led past Llanwnda and down to Fishguard, but to leave the path and try to climb to the lane through the tangle of overgrown rocks and thickets would be foolish. He held on by the path, slowing to a steady trot and able now to think of the implications of what he had heard from St Leger.

If Tate was suing for terms it meant that Fishguard was safe. The Black Legion's invasion had ended in fiasco, thanks to the miraculous speed with which Colonel Knox and Lord Cawdor and the rest of the authorities had mustered superior forces to oppose it. Or could it be –

He had checked suddenly as a wide prospect burst upon him. The little path had made a steep descent followed by a steeper climb to the pointed summit of a rocky tor, whose heathery ledges provided couches for a few sheep. It was an exposed spot to stand and get his breath, but he was far round the hillside and out of sight of the place where he had left his captors, which was a good mile astern. Mr Fitton, from his perch some 500 feet above sea-level, saw Fishguard for the first time.

The ground fell away very steeply from his feet to the hidden nearer shore of the bay, and he commanded a bird's-eye view of all that lay beyond. The blue waters of the bay glittered in spring-like sunshine and a small vessel – it was *Curlew* – was anchored off the point, but to the right the bay's head was a wide expanse of golden sand, at the farther side of which was the little harbour and the port. The white and grey houses of the town clung round the middle and lower slopes of a conical hill, and he could just see, at the head of the sands, the bridge and the road that led up into Fishguard. It was a colourful picture; and it was a moment or two before he perceived that the picture was crammed with human figures.

Directly below him, ranged along the uneven terraces of turf and rock above the shore, were the motionless black ranks of French soldiers, seen only in part because of intervening crags and thickets. Across the sands, perhaps a mile and a half away, the paths or lanes on the slope below the town were lined with red-and-white dots, and more of these dots were moving in an endless

Quixote at Fishguard

line down a road that slanted into the town across the side of the conical hill. Massed at the edge of the sands, below the houses, were rows of blue-and-white figures, unmistakably the militia detachment; he thought there might be two or three hundred men. A little way in front of them three men sat on horseback, and as he watched two of the horsemen began to canter across the sand towards the Black Legion's position, one of them carrying a white flag on a pole. He took out his glass and watched them until they passed from his sight under the projection of the hillside below him; they wore the blue-and-white of the Fishguard Fencibles but he didn't think either of them was Colonel Knox. He turned his glass on the town.

It was not often that Mr Fitton's customarily expressionless face wore a broad grin but it did so now. The deception tickled his sense of humour. Even through the lens those long stiff ranks of St Leger's 'bloody redcoats' looked impressive with their red-and-white and the black grenadier hats, but every one of them was a Welshwoman in red shawl and white *brat*. And that seemingly endless procession of counterfeit infantrymen marching down into the town was, he felt certain, literally endless – it curled unseen round the back of the conical hill, marching round and down again. Someone had adopted and bettered the unlikely plan he had dispatched to Fishguard by Sam Evans.

He took a brief look at *Curlew* before returning the glass to his pocket. Mr Tibbs had contrived a jury topmast, he saw; perhaps with one of the long sweeps she carried. And Barrington would certainly have come ashore. His own course now was to get himself, with his sore feet and torn breeches and ragged stockings, to Fishguard to report to his captain.

The morning was well advanced and there was warmth in the pale sunlight as he sought and found a sheep-track that seemed to head in the direction he wanted. It brought him down and up again to a stone wall and a gate, and across a steep field to another gate giving onto a lane. The lane ran down very steeply, passing a cottage or two and several barns, but there was no one about in field or garden, and when he had at last come down to sea-level and the head of Goodwick Sands he saw why. Every man and woman and child for miles around must have congregated in Fishguard and its approach road. Carts, wagons, horses and people thronged the narrow causeway before the short ascent to the houses at its end, and all were talking loudly with their attention fixed on the sands where the men of the militia were countermarching and forming rank with an officer or two cantering about them. The talk that came to his ears as he pushed his way through the crowds and up into the equally crowded streets was mainly unintelligible to him, being in Welsh, but here and there an English voice spoke excitedly of surrender or declared that the Frogs ought to be shot every man. In the little central square the clamour and the press were even greater, especially before the long low tavern that filled most of one side. Its sign proclaimed it the Royal Oak.

For the moment Mr Fitton could see no easy way of getting near the door of the Royal Oak. The mob that jostled and chattered between him and the door was composed of excited countryfolk – farmers and shepherds, grooms and ploughmen, mothers with broods of children – and it was just now being pressed closer by the passage through it of what seemed to be a small procession. Half a dozen laughing Welsh girls in tall hats and red shawls were pushing through with a very tall woman, similarly dressed, in their midst. The little man who was standing beside Mr Fitton, a small tradesman by his apron, jogged an elbow into his ribs.

'*Diawl*, she's the fine one!' he shouted above the din of voices. 'Jemima Nicholas, that is – brought in a dozen

Frenchies prisoner with her pitchfork! They're off down to the cliff path,' he added. 'Come on – we'll see the armies from there!'

He burrowed into the crowd without waiting for an answer. Others were moving in the wake of the girls and the mob was thinning. Mr Fitton could see five or six saddled horses tied to the long hitching-rail to the right of the inn and noted now the self-conscious militia sentry at its door; this was military headquarters and he might find Barrington here. He had started to cross the square when there was a clatter of hooves and an officer in blue-and-white came riding up with scant regard for the folk in his way. He reined-in at the inn door, threw himself off his horse, and dashed inside, leaving the sentry to hold his mount's bridle.

The crowd that still remained in the square pressed up to the front of the inn in noisy excitement. Mr Fitton hesitated. He might not find himself very welcome if he pushed in with his inquiry just as some important dispatch arrived. But hardly a minute had passed when three men came out to stand in the inn porch, and one of the three was the commander of the *Curlew*. One of the others, a tall man in a green uniform and white breeches, spoke at once, at the top of his voice, at first in Welsh and then in English. The uproar of cheers and shouts that followed his first sentence almost drowned the English version.

'The French have surrendered – unconditionally!'

Mr Fitton stepped forward but Barrington had already plunged through the rejoicing crowd and was shaking him by the hand. His bony face was flushed and he was plainly wildly excited.

'Gad's me life!' he exclaimed. 'Fitton, by God! Where the devil have you been, man? – But you can tell it to Lord Cawdor – he's the general officer commanding and he's within there now. I'll bring you to him.'

'By your leave, sir, I'm in no fit state –'

'To hell with your looks! 'Twas your plan, as Evans tells me, that turned the scale for us, and Cawdor's heard of it. Come on!'

He turned and made for the inn door, Mr Fitton following.

'Cawdor's had our part of the tale too,' Barrington threw over his shoulder as they went, 'not forgetting your Madame Spy. He's a magistrate and he'll have a warrant out for her arrest tomorrow morning.'

They had passed the sentry who was still holding the bridle of the officer's horse. In the porch Barrington halted.

'Best heave-to here while I see if Lord Cawdor's disengaged,' he said, and vanished at once into the inn.

Without a second's hesitation Mr Fitton turned on his heel and twitched the bridle from the sentry's hand.

'This beast needs fodder,' he said sharply. 'I'll see to it.'

The man goggled at him but made no demur. He led the horse quickly past the row of horses at the hitching-rail. People were still passing through the square on their way to the town's sea-front and he stopped a middle-aged man who looked like a farmer.

'The Haverfordwest road, if you please.'

'Why, 'tis fifty yards up, on the right!' the man told him, astonished that anyone should be so ignorant.

Mr Fitton cast one glance behind him. The sentry was staring after him from the inn porch, but Barrington had not reappeared. He swung himself into the saddle and kicked his steed into a trot. At the right-hand turn between the houses there was a signpost, HAVERFORD-WEST 14. As he took this road he urged the horse into a canter.

2

In acting as he did Mr Fitton had wantonly jettisoned all the careful teachings of his philosophy, without giving a thought to his apostasy. *Before undertaking an enterprise, look well to its end* – Epictetus, or Mr Fitton's Tutelary Genius, would have been shocked by his utter disregard of that wise advice. He had shut his eyes to any end beyond Long Warren, and saw only the arraignment and penalty that awaited Simone de Callac.

It was clear that time was important. If she was to be arrested tomorrow morning as Barrington had stated, there was much less than a day's grace for her flight. How she would arrange that he didn't know, but the sooner she could be warned the more chance she would have of escape. A transient sense of his own foolishness did make itself felt as the last cottages of Fishguard fell behind him, but he thrust it firmly from him and rode on with his immediate purpose unshaken. He came to a turnpike cottage but the pole was raised and the keeper absent, no doubt in Fishguard with everyone else. Beyond the turnpike the metalled road ran unfenced with a verge of turf on which he could for a time maintain a gallop. The animal he had taken was Hobson's choice and he was fortunate to bestride a mare as docile as this – she had accepted a strange rider without a tremor – but she was no cavalry charger; presumably the officers of the Fishguard Fencibles, not being yeomanry, had to rely on what they could get in the way of horseflesh. The mare was a gaunt and rawboned beast that reminded Mr Fitton of Rosinante. The comparison, however, went no further in his mind.

Long Warren, Sam Evans had said, was seven miles south of Fishguard; he might do that in forty minutes. But soon the road, which had run almost level across pastures, dipped to cross a stream and thereafter ran between hedges with ditches in place of the turf verge. Galloping on the flints of the road surface was good neither for horse nor rider, for Mr Fitton's horsemanship was not up to coping with a stumble or a fall. He rode less urgently, curbing his impatience.

He met no one until he had ridden four miles. Then, as he descended the hill to a bridge over a side-stream, he saw a troop of horsemen in dark-blue uniforms with white facings trotting down the opposing hill. The officer at the head of the troop hailed him as he approached.

'New Romney Dragoons – what news of the French?'

'They've surrendered,' Mr Fitton told him.

The man – he was young and wondrously whiskered – flung his arms wide. 'May the devil blast the bastards!' he cried angrily. 'We've been riding all day! Why couldn't they wait for us?'

He pushed past with his troop and Mr Fitton resumed his hurried journey. Though it was past noon the day had lost its brightness. Grey cloud had spread across the sky and the east wind, so long the maintainer of weather unseasonably fine and dry, had sharpened to a wintry chill. Mr Fitton shivered as he rode down a long straight hill with his eyes on a cluster of stone cottages at the bottom of the hill and a lane that emerged from the slopes on his left to join the road there. There were weird fingers of crag stabbing the grey sky from a hilltop above it. This was undoubtedly Wolf's Castle, which he had last seen a fortnight ago. And then he saw the chaise. It came bumping along the lane from the direction of Long Warren. With an odd leap of the heart he struck heels into his Rosinante's flanks and cantered down to intercept it at the corner.

The chaise was drawn by a single horse and the man riding it, he saw as he drew nearer, was Madame de Callac's groom, Gaston. At sight of the approaching horseman Gaston drew rein, but a moment later the chaise moved on and reached the junction of lane and road precisely as Mr Fitton pulled his horse to a standstill, blocking the way. A glance showed him the baggage lashed on the roof, Madame's face at the window, and Gaston half-turned in his saddle with a pistol in his hand. Disregarding the pistol, he dismounted and went to the window, which had been lowered. Her maid was with her but he saw only the blue-grey eyes that regarded him so steadily.

'*Enfin*, Mr Fitton, we meet for a second time,' she said pleasantly. 'I am setting out, as you see, to do my marketing in Haverfordwest. You were intending to call on me, perhaps?'

Her dark hair was covered with some filmy grey material and a small ringlet had escaped to lie on the curve of her cheek. Mr Fitton found it hard to speak, and when he did speak his voice emerged harsh and toneless.

'I have ridden from Fishguard, Madame. The French under General Tate have surrendered. It is known to the British command that you are a French agent.'

He had expected her to flinch, to cry an indignant denial. But she did neither. Her gaze did not waver and when she spoke her voice was steady.

'And you believe that?'

'I know it for the truth, Madame,' he answered.

'You rode hither to tell me this?'

'I came to warn you, Madame. You are to be arrested tomorrow morning.'

'To warn me?' she repeated, her eyes widening. 'But – but surely, sir, in doing so you have betrayed your country.'

Mr Fitton reddened. 'My country does not make war on women,' he said stiffly.

She frowned, hesitated, started to speak and checked herself. In the slight shrug of her shoulders he read acceptance of her exposure.

'I have to thank you, sir,' she said evenly. 'But you must know that I would not have stayed to let myself be taken. Gaston was in Fishguard this morning. He rode in half an hour ago with the news that Tate had asked for terms, and my preparations were made. Gwennie and Sarah are in Fishguard and Long Warren is empty.' She paused. 'I am sorry – yes, sorry – to leave it. But I shall be in France two days from now.'

'But how will you –'

She stopped him with a small hand upraised. For the first time there was a faint smile on her lips.

'You will not expect me to tell you that, Mr Fitton. I knew that if Tate failed and was taken, Simone de Callac would cease to exist. For me there would be arrest, and an English prison or worse. For he will talk, that one. I know his sort.' There was scorn in her tone. 'While their clever schemes go well they are heroes, but let disaster fall and they grovel in the dust. They are like M. Montgolfier's balloon, grandly puffed up until they are pricked, then – *pouf*!'

'Why do you ally yourself with such a man?' he demanded abruptly.

She tilted her chin and her eyes flashed. 'Because I obey my orders, sir! Because I cannot use a sword! You fight for your country – I fight for France in the only way I can.'

Mr Fitton remembered the demagogues of the Directory that ruled France and was puzzled.

'But surely you, an aristocrat, must see –' he began...

'I, an aristocrat!' she broke in on a note of mockery. 'Mr Fitton, did you not hear me say that Simone de Callac has ceased to exist?'

He understood her. 'Who are you, then?' he muttered.

She laughed. 'You will not have heard of me but in Paris I am known. Ask at the Comédie Française – the stage-door, if you please – and they will recite for you the stage triumphs of Suzanne Leclos.'

Gaston, who had put his pistol back into his pocket, gave an inarticulate growl and she threw a *Bien sûr!* at him. When her eyes returned to Mr Fitton they were kind.

'We must go,' she said. 'This time, sir, it is *adieu pour toujours* and – I am sorry. You will forget me, but I shall remember what you did – for me. You will accept the thanks of Suzanne Leclos?'

She extended her hand through the window as she spoke. Mr Fitton took it and pressed it to his lips. Gaston shook his reins, the window was drawn up, and the chaise rumbled past him into the Haverfordwest road.

Mr Fitton stood watching it as it gathered speed and disappeared round the wooded bend of the hill below Wolf's Castle. When it had gone he stood there still, for perhaps two minutes. Then he turned, and climbing somewhat stiffly into the saddle set his horse's head towards Fishguard.

3

The southerly wind with its thin driving rain was over *Curlew*'s larboard bow as she headed sou'-west, close-hauled, to weather St David's Head. Mr Fitton, astraddle on her little quarterdeck with his tarpaulin coat glistening wet with spray, looked astern for a last glimpse of Strumble Head, a grey hump looming through the rain veil. The weather had changed at last. If this wind held it would be fair for Plymouth once the Lizard had been rounded, but it was making the cutter labour.

'Bear away half-a-point,' he said to Evans at the helm.

'Half-a-point, sir.'

'Steady as she goes. – Well, Mr Tibbs?'

The carpenter had come aft along the sloping deck, his bald head swathed in a yellow scarf.

'She's not let in more'n an inch, sir,' he said with some pride. 'Barring a gale and high seas, we'll fetch Plymouth without using the pump.'

'You made a good job of it.'

'Well enough, sir, well enough. And if them lazy hounds at Plymouth dockyard knows how to fit a fathom o' scantling she should be ready for sea again in three days.'

He departed for'ard, where the boatswain was busy with a party flaking down the anchor-cables. Mr Fitton bethought him of something and stepped nearer the helm.

'By the by, Sam,' he said, 'Gwennie Jones has left Long Warren. She was in Fishguard the morning of the surrender.'

Sam grinned. 'I knows it, sir. I was ashore then an' I picked Gwennie out o' the crowd, like.'

'You were able to give her a bit of comfort, I hope?'

'Aye, sir, I was that. She's a good little wench is Gwennie but she needs looking after,' he added with a touch of defiance.

'And maybe you're the man for that?'

Before Sam could reply the cutter's captain had come on deck. Barrington threw a rapid glance at the trim of the sail and then raised his voice in a shout.

'Mr Masters! Take over the deck, if you please! – Mr Fitton,' he added, turning, 'oblige me by coming below for a moment.'

Mr Fitton followed him down to the captain's cabin. Barrington gestured him to a chair at the table and sat down himself. He seemed less at ease than usual and his first words sounded a trifle forced.

'It's good to be at sea again, by God! A feller don't feel free ashore – though I'll wager the Black Legion'll feel a deal less free afloat in the Portsmouth prison-hulks.'

He stopped and rubbed his chin, glancing askance at his subordinate. Mr Fitton felt bound to break an awkward silence.

'Tate and his officers are to be taken to London, sir, I believe.'

'I'd have shot 'em out of hand,' Barrington said; he seemed to make up his mind. 'See here, Fitton, you're due for a reprimand from me. It's no good your sitting there like a wooden image – you can't deny it. When I think what –' He paused and suddenly chuckled. 'Gad's me life, but you've chalked up a list! Absenting yourself without leave, stealing a horse, holding converse with the King's enemies – by God, there's enough to hang you!'

Mr Fitton said nothing. Barrington leaned across the table and addressed him more seriously.

'Your part in this business earned you a recommendation, but that's gone down the wind. Knox and Lord Cawdor listened to the yarn Evans primed me with – that you'd taken it into your head to carry the news to Evans's uncle at Letterston – but I could see with half an eye they didn't believe it. Nobody would. I doubt they'll carry it further, but there'll be no praise for you in their report. So there'll be no help towards your commission this time.'

It had not occurred to Mr Fitton that his doings might bring him nearer to the coveted step in rank, and the news that they wouldn't did not greatly dismay him. Barrington, who was eyeing him curiously, asked a sudden question.

'Was she a pretty woman, this French madame of yours?'

Mr Fitton took a moment to answer. 'I found her – attractive,' he said at last, without expression.

Barrington grinned. 'I don't doubt it. By God, I'd give a month's pay to have met her! And mark this, Fitton – there'll be no mention of your meeting her in my log.'

'Thank you, sir.'

'I'm no hypocrite – I'd have done the same myself,

d'ye see.' He got up and took bottle and glasses from the bulkhead cupboard. 'We'll drink to her.'

Curlew lifted her bows on a wave as they drank that toast and Barrington set down his half-empty glass carefully.

'We'll have some shootin' at Plymouth, Fitton,' he said. 'There's two estuaries there, and we'll take the boat up. The season's over, but only by a day or two, and this time I'll bring down a bird or bust – teal, pochard, mallard, anything.'

'Anything,' said Mr Fitton, 'but a homing pigeon.'

Author's Note

In case the reader is not aware of it, the 'invasion' by the Black Legion under Colonel Tate did in fact take place, much as described in this story.